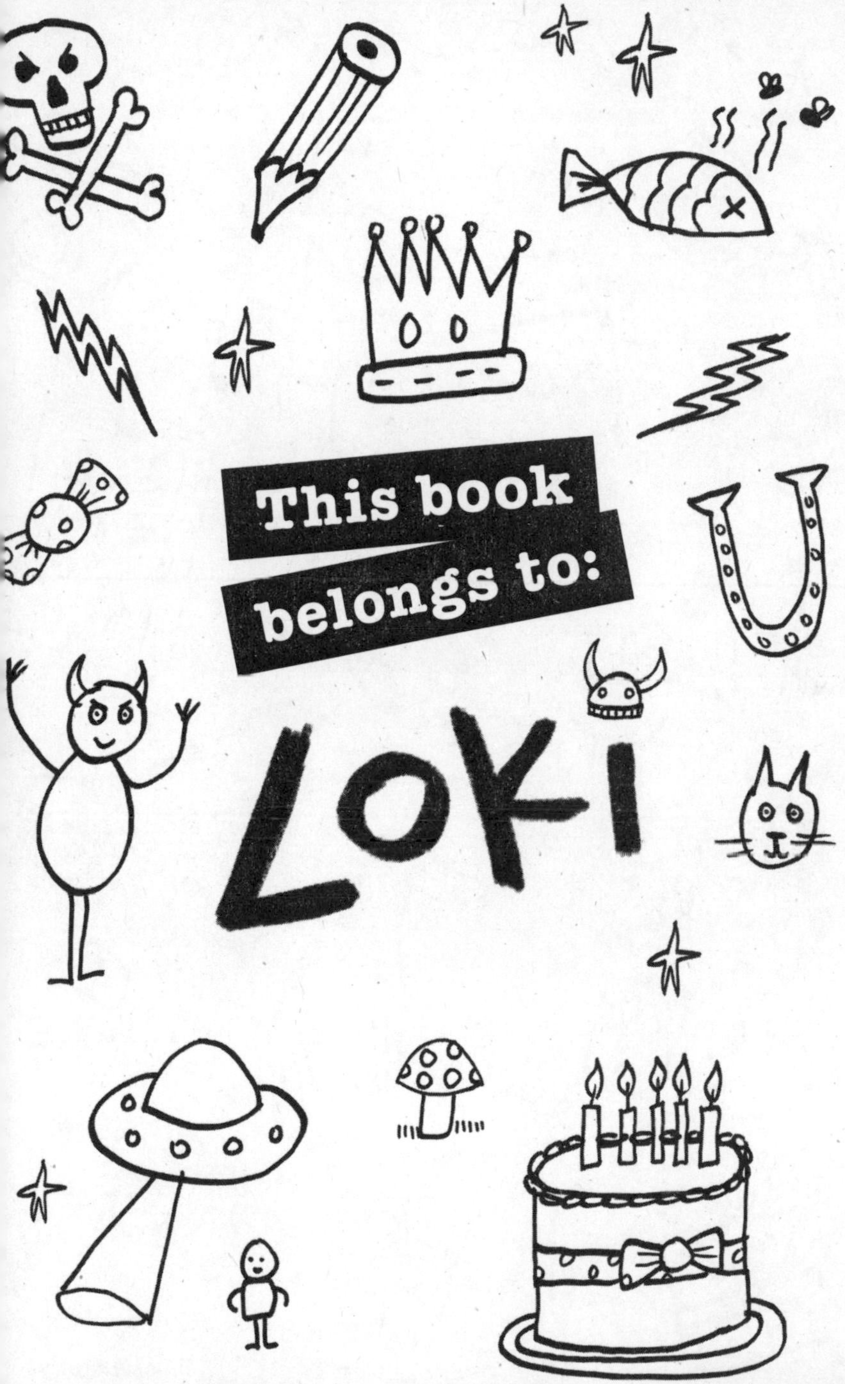
This book
belongs to:
LOKI

SPELLS
CHIPS

OWELL

LOKI

A BAD GOD'S GUIDE TO TAKING THE BLAME

WALKER BOOKS

This is a work of fiction.
Names, characters, places, and incidents are either products of the author's imagination or, if real, are used fictitiously.

First US edition 2023

Library of Congress Catalog Card Number 2022915241
ISBN 978-1-5362-2630-0

23 24 25 26 27 28 LBM 10 9 8 7 6 5 4 3 2 1

Printed in Melrose Park, IL, USA

This book was typeset in Autumn Voyage, Avenir, Bembo, Blackout, Cabazon, ITC American Typewriter, Liquid Embrace, Neato Serif, OpenSans, Times, and WB Loki.
The illustrations were done in pen.

Walker Books US
a division of
Candlewick Press
99 Dover Street
Somerville, Massachusetts 02144

www.walkerbooksus.com

FSC
www.fsc.org
MIX
Paper | Supporting responsible forestry
FSC® C103098

To the creators of my universe, Jean and Frank

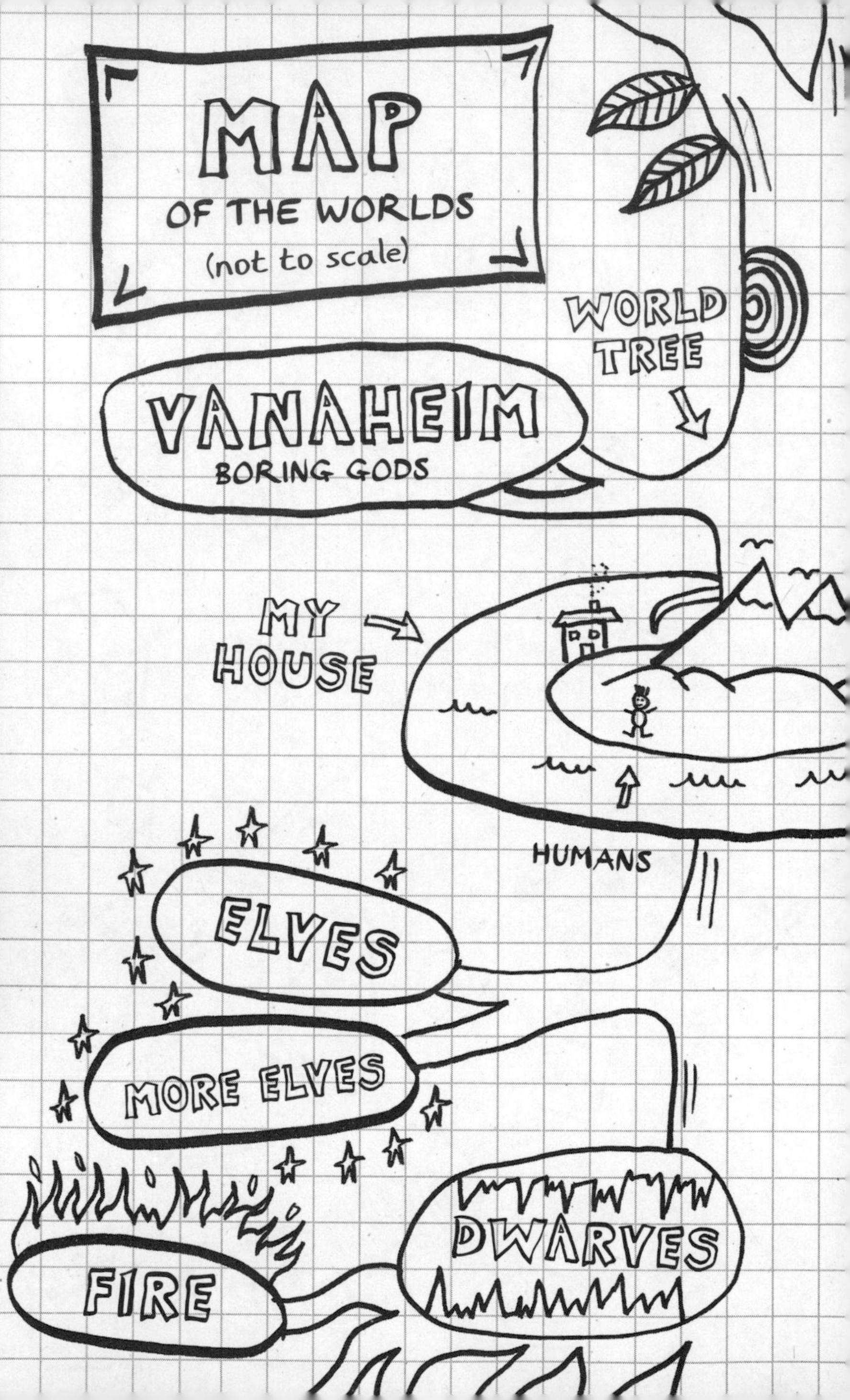
MAP
OF THE WORLDS
(not to scale)
WORLD TREE
VANAHEIM
BORING GODS
MY HOUSE
HUMANS
ELVES
MORE ELVES
DWARVES
FIRE

EXCITING GODS
FANCY PALACES
ASGARD
MIDGARD
RAINBOW BRIDGE
THE WORLD SERPENT
FISH
JOTUNHEIM
GIANTS LIVE HERE
DEAD PEOPLE
HEL
ICE

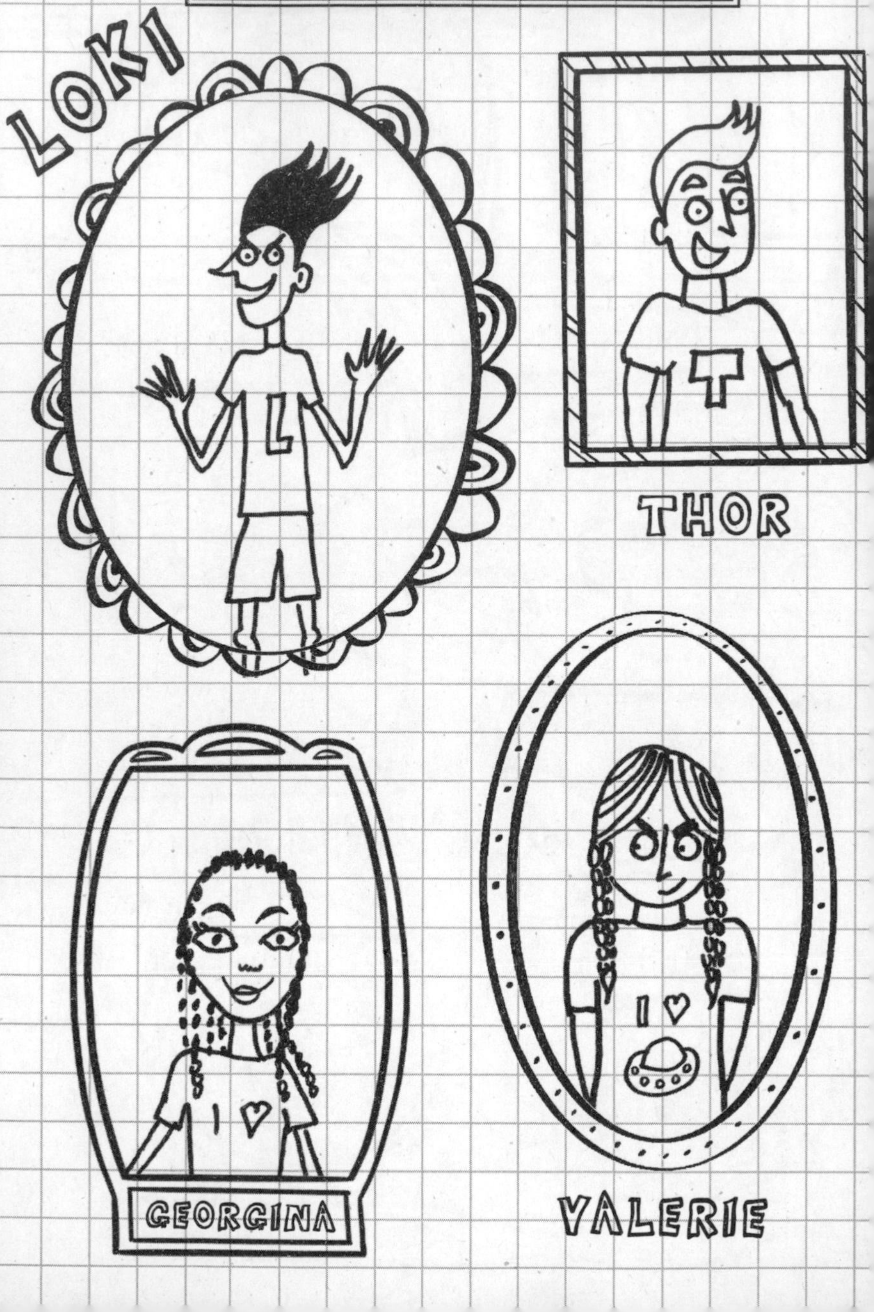
The Characters
LOKI
L
THOR
T
GEORGINA
I ♥
VALERIE
I ♥

FIDO
HEIMDALL
SARAH
HYRROKKIN
ODIN
SPORTSBOY ONE

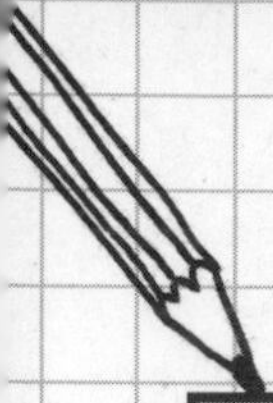

Class Schedule

	Monday	Tuesday
1	MATH	MATH
BREAK		
2	ART	LANGUAGE ARTS
3	SPELLING	ENGLISH
LUNCH		
4	SOCIAL STUDIES	GEOGRAPHY
5	PE	SCIENCE

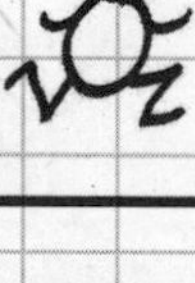

LOKI ♡s LUNCH BREAK

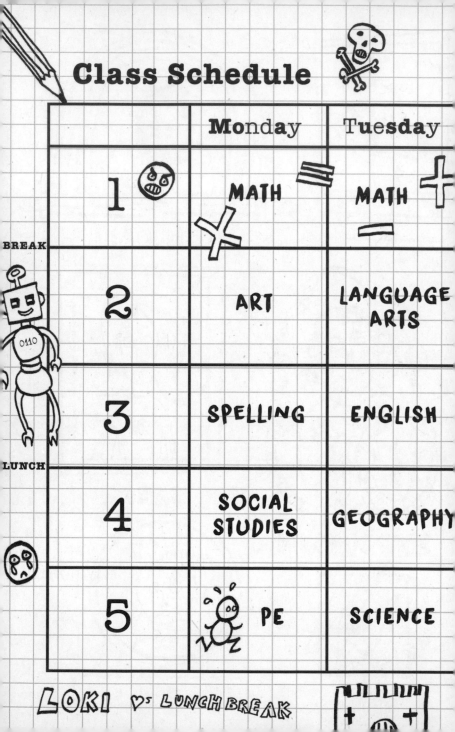

Wednesday	Thursday	Friday
DRAMA	SPELLING	ENGLISH
ENGLISH	LANGUAGE ARTS	MUSIC
COMPUTING	HEALTH	FRENCH
MATH	ART	PE
FRENCH	SOCIAL STUDIES	HISTORY

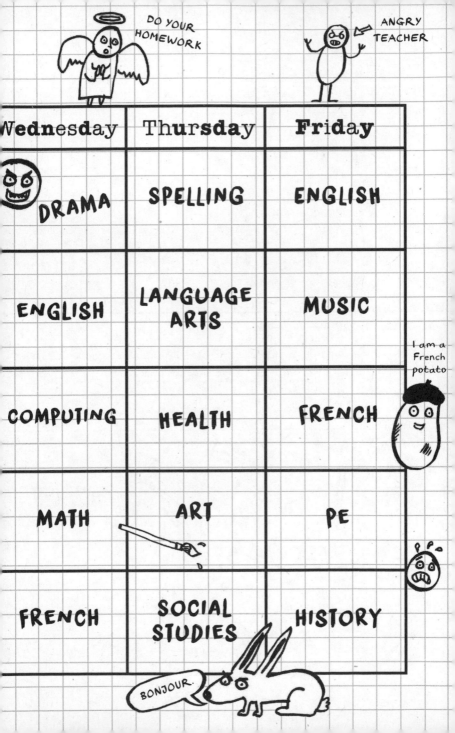

FART

About This Book

My name is Loki, and I am a god.

Sort of.

It's complicated.

These days, I'm living on Midgard (aka Earth to you) in the form of a puny mortal boy named Liam.

I still possess the powers of a mighty god, but I'm forbidden from revealing them. Also, I have to go to school.

None suffer like I suffer.

But let's just say: it could have been worse. Allow me to catch you up . . .

I cut off the goddess Sif's hair as a prank.
LOL.
GRR.
ME
SIF
ASGARD
Me
Off to Midgard, Trickster!
MIDGARD
Then . . .
Mortalify
Enyoungen
You must become good!
Gulp
And keep an honest record of your deeds . . .
BONK
Diary
OR ELSE.

Thor came as my "brother."
I'm watching you, Loki.
And Hyrrokkin and Heimdall came as my "parents."
I discovered mortal life is BRUTAL and CRUEL.
School
AHHH!
RAAAH!
Students
Teachers
Then I fought Frost Giants and WON.
Oh no, I am defeated!
And something wonderful happened . . . I made a (mortal) friend!
Me
Valerie AKA Best Friend
THE END.

! Except that wasn't the end, was it, Loki?

Argh. Do you have to correct every tiny embroidery of the truth?

! Yes. It's the entire point of this diary.

BAH. Well, you should get a hobby.

So, OK, it wasn't the end of my story. Even after all that heroism, I still have to stay on Earth and keep writing in this ridiculous diary. It gives me points when I do good things and takes points away when I do . . . less good things. I have to do all this until I become "worthy of Asgard." Whatever that means.

On top of this, I have a new mission: to protect the mortal realm from Frost Giants and other unpleasant characters from the realms beyond this one.

Now that we're all caught up, on with the Loki Show!

Day One

Monday

LOKI VIRTUE SCORE OR LVS:

0

Reset for a fresh start

Better than the minus millions, I suppose!

Today at school, I performed a mighty feat: I was nice to the new kid.

If you've never attended a mortal school, you might not know that it is a long-standing tradition that the new child in class is treated with disdain and cruelty.

However, because I am a Good God™ now, I ignored this custom, risking the scorn of my peers!

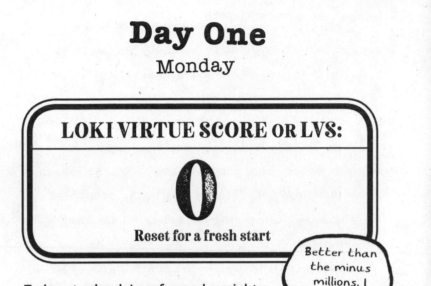

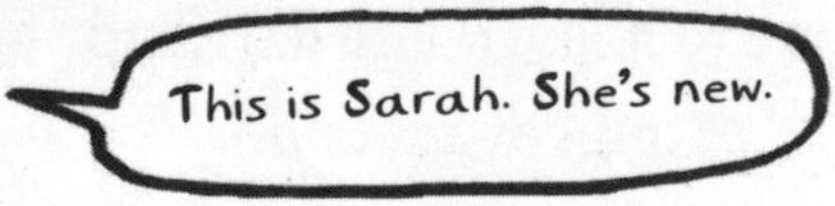

This is Sarah. She's new.

"Miss, Sarah can sit next to me," I said, gesturing graciously at an empty chair beside me.

Thor, who was sitting on my other side, leaned over. "What did you do to her chair? Spread peanut butter over the seat? Or superglue?"

"Nothing!" I promised.

> ! **No lie detected.**

"Actually," said Sarah, "I'd rather sit over there if that's OK?" She pointed at a chair far, far away from me.

I sat there with my mouth open in horror as Sarah trotted to her new seat. I had done this noble deed, driven by pity for a poor unfortunate soul, and . . . she refused my offer? She turned down Loki? ME?

Well. I don't know why I bother.

> ! **You bother because you want to become a good person in order to be allowed to return home to Asgard one day. And you still have a LOT of improving to do.**

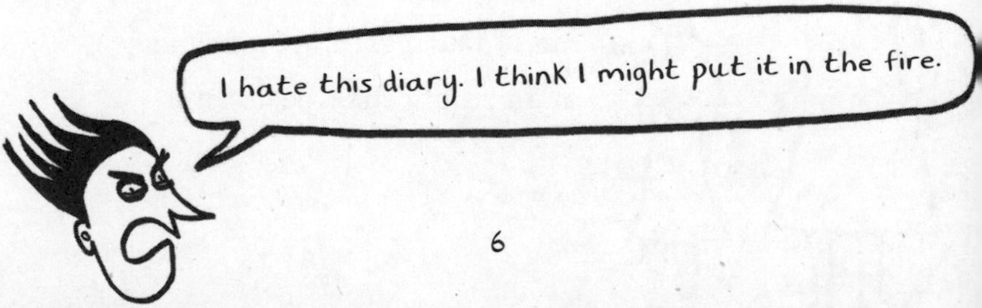

I hate this diary. I think I might put it in the fire.

I'm flame-retardant to the highest temperatures of the fiery wilderness of Muspelheim. !

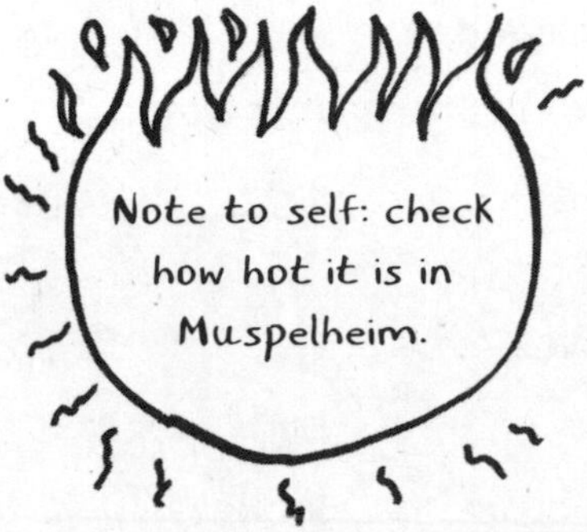

After school, I watched TV with Thor and Hyrrokkin. Heimdall was busy installing what mortals call an alarm.

Alarm: a device that emits a high-pitched sound when thieves break into your house. Also prone to beeping at random intervals for no reason, especially in the middle of the night.

When I come across an unfamiliar mortal concept, this book shows me an explanation written by "all-knowing" Odin himself. Sometimes it sounds like he's just making fun of mortals.

"Who would want to break into this pathetic hovel anyway?" I asked.

"Giants!" said Heimdall.

"And what do we have that the giants would want to steal?" I asked, gesturing around at the drab mortal dwelling that we call home. Not a gold throne or a diamond-encrusted chalice in sight, unlike in Asgard.

"They might want to steal Thor's hammer!" said Heimdall. "Or kidnap one of us! Or steal"—he cast his eyes around the room—"our television. It's very large. Anyway. Dinnertime. Go and wash your hands. With soap!"

After dinner, Hyrrokkin fed her snakes. While she was busy popping dead mice into the eager mouths of serpents, Thor and I did chores.

Chores are one of the cruelest parts of being a mortal child. Especially today's horrifying task:

LOKI – Tidy that mess of a bedroom!

THOR – Dust hammer collection—
your bedroom is already tidy.

In Asgard, if you drop something, it magically returns itself to its proper place. But tragically that does not happen in the mortal realm.

Apparently, my system for storing my belongings was not acceptable to my fake parents. I don't know why. I know where everything is.

I'm quite annoyed that Thor is so good at cleaning his room. In fact, I think he only does it to annoy me.

He came to bother me after dusting his hammers. As I worked my tender fingers to the bone, he went on and on about how funny it was that the new girl turned down my offer of a seat. I don't believe Thor truly grasps the concept of humor. Humiliation is only funny when it's not happening to me.

"I think it was very rude of her," I said haughtily.

"That's why it was funny," said Thor. "Though not as funny as your face when she turned you down like a friendless loser."

Just before I wreaked terrible vengeance upon Thor, thereby destroying my status as a Good God™, Hyrrokkin called us downstairs.

"I have received an email from your school," she said, frowning.

Hyrrokkin disapproves of emails. In fact, she considers paper letters to be newfangled and prefers runes etched into stone, or at least painted on a "nice bit of vellum."

"The school is to hold a mystical ritual on Thursday, in which you will be judged," she went on. "Your teachers will tell Heimdall and me if you have proved worthy."

But how will my teachers know if I am worthy? I have not completed any quests to show my worth!

Hyrrokkin explained that the mystical ritual was something called a parents' night, and that our worthiness would be judged based on how "Liam" (me) and "Thomas" (Thor) have performed at school.

While I know that I am a delight to be around and a wit of the highest order, the thought of being judged by my teachers did give me a strange feeling in my stomach.

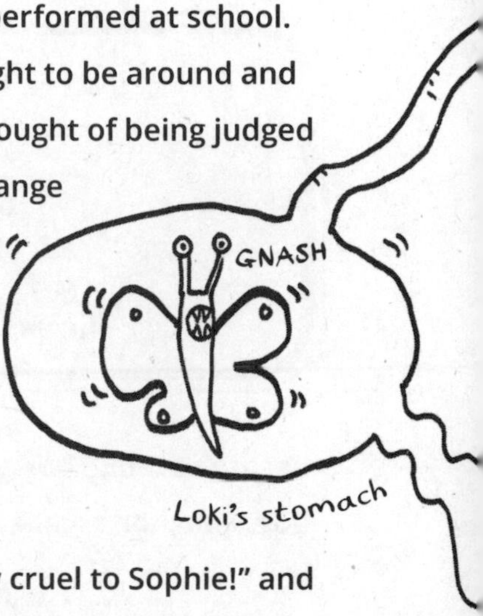
GNASH
Loki's stomach

You see, sometimes my genius can be misconstrued. Teachers have been known to shout at me, saying things like "Liam, don't disrupt the class!" and "Liam, stop being needlessly cruel to Sophie!" and "Oh God, why did they have to put you in my class? Does the principal hate me?"

But I dismissed my worries. After all, what does it matter what my teachers say about me at this paltry meeting in three days' time? I am an immortal god, glorious and mighty! I do not need their praise.

You need everybody's praise, Loki. You're incredibly insecure.

!
Have I mentioned that I hate this diary?

Day Two

Tuesday

LOKI VIRTUE SCORE OR LVS:

50

For offering the new girl a seat

That WAS kind of me, yes.

Before school, Thor and I took Hyrrokkin's dog, Fido, for a walk.

Actually a giant wolf in disguise.
Poop comes out of here frequently.

While we were out, we bumped into my best mortal friend, Valerie, who was wearing a strange black helmet.

Once upon a time, I would have kicked Thor in the shins for talking about god business, but Valerie knows the truth. (OK, I told her. For heroic reasons.)

"War? No . . . I'm going to the riding stables before school." She leaned closer. "But do gods go to war often? I'd love to hear more about it—"

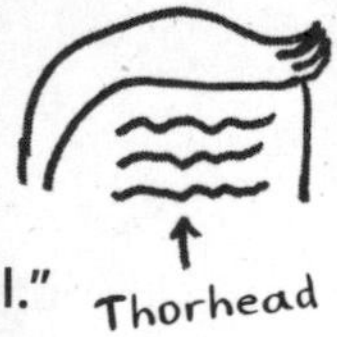

"Wait . . ." Thor furrowed his stupidly handsome forehead. "No! You know too much already, mortal."

"She is no mere mortal," I objected. "She is Valerie Kerry, best friend of Loki!"

"The dog has deposited feces on the ground. It is your turn to pick it up," said Thor, interrupting our very touching moment of friendship.

So Valerie went off to the stables while I scooped dog poop from the ground with only a bag between my divine hand and the excrement.

Mortal life is *gross*.

At school, during break, I chatted with Valerie. I had hoped that we could discuss my magnificence, but instead of asking me questions about myself and hanging on my every word (as I deserve), she talked about a girl she'd met at the stables that morning.

Her name's Georgina and she's amazing. She's in the other class at school, so you wouldn't know her. She's been riding almost as long as I have! She doesn't like aliens—which is a shame—but I really like her. She's into coding and she's so pretty and she's really good with horses, and she can do jumps! Oh, and the new owner of the stables said Georgina was the best rider she'd seen in years!

Valerie said all this in such a breathless rush, I feared that she might suffocate. Georgina was clearly very bad for Valerie.

Surely she is not as good with horses as I, Loki?

"Better!" said Valerie.

"But . . . I *was* a horse!" I objected.

"Yes, but just because you've *been* a horse doesn't mean you know how to *ride* a horse. That's like saying because you've been a cow, you know how to milk it."

(I actually lived underground for eight years milking cows professionally. Long story. I'll tell you when I'm not trying to prove myself against a mysterious and intriguing stranger.)

"Anyway, I think you'd really like her. She's so interesting and funny and smart," said Valerie.

Valerie went on and on and on about Georgina, and I started to feel a little unwell. Would Valerie ever *stop* talking? Surely she risked straining her throat muscles?

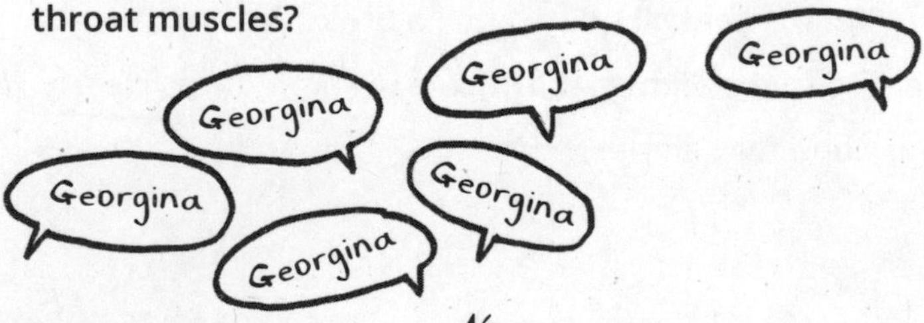

". . . and guess what?"

"She can also fly and fart rainbows?" I said sullenly.

"No! She was in Mrs. Williams's class last year! We have so much in common!" Valerie looked delighted by this not-exactly-a-coincidence, given that there are only a limited number of teachers in our school.

Mrs. Williams is our teacher. I don't like to dignify teachers with names, but I reluctantly confess that I know them.

This was not the enjoyable break time I had hoped for. Valerie was abandoning me for a mere mortal! She's *my* friend. As with Thor's hammer: if someone else takes it, it would not be *his* hammer anymore. This Georgina was committing daylight friend robbery!

What I wanted to say was

What I actually said, through gritted teeth, was "I'd love to meet her."

"I'm sure she'd love to meet you, too! I've told her all about you. Well, not the god stuff obviously," said Valerie.

Stupid oath to Odin, making it harder to show how cool I am. (I swore an oath that I would not reveal my mighty godly powers to mortals. While I got away with breaking this oath once, I suspect Odin would not be as forgiving if I did it again.)

"I'm sure she'll like you anyway," Valerie went on. "Georgina's so kind, she likes *everyone*."

Everyone? That word landed like a blow to the stomach with a very large and knobbly giant's club. I'm not just anyone! I'm adorable! People love me because *I* am awesome, not because *they* are kind! I need nobody's pity—nor their secondhand friends!

I made a silent vow.

So, instead of sitting next to Valerie in English, I put my pencil case down next to the new girl, Sarah. This is a universal symbol that mortal children use to show that a seat is now theirs.

MINE! Trespassers will be prosecuted.

But when I returned from gathering a sheet of paper from the front, I was horrified to discover that Sarah had moved my pencil case to another seat.

For a moment, my heart filled with bile.

How DARE she reject me?

Then I had an idea that made much more sense than her deeming me unworthy of friendship. It was probably her humility that made her move my pencil case, thinking she was not worthy of being so close to one as special as I. Giving her a reassuring smile, I sat down next to her anyway.

Clearly overcome by my generosity, she slumped forward onto her arms with an enormous sigh.

Then she sat up straight and raised her hand.

Mrs. Williams made me return to sit with Valerie, the one person I could rely upon to receive me with joy and gratitude! But as I took my seat, she didn't even look up. Her attention was completely focused on the drawing she was doing of a girl riding a horse.

It was a very good drawing and truly a shame that it fell on the floor at the end of the lesson and got trampled by the class as they left the classroom.

And how DID it fall? !

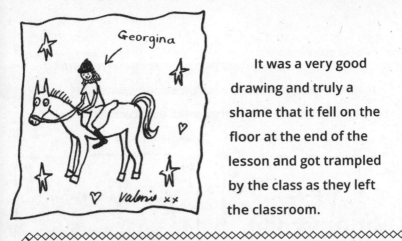

That's what I thought. Leaving out some of the truth is a form of lying, you know. !

PAH!

No it's not. If you put every single detail in a story, it would be terribly dull!

After school, I walked home with Thor. On a wall near our house someone had stuck up some posters that contained a number of pleas and commands.

Visit Sunnyville!
It has good food and attractive people, unlike your pathetic excuse for a town!

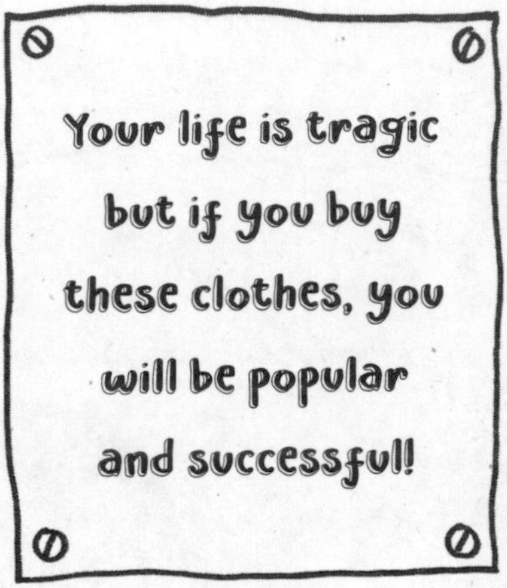

Your life is tragic but if you buy these clothes, you will be popular and successful!

WHY BUY A HAMMER WHEN YOU CAN JOIN HAMMERSWAP?
EXCHANGE YOUR OLD HAMMERS FOR BRAND-NEW ONES—
ALL FREE!

At first, I thought they might be some kind of mortal code of moral conduct, but then I remembered they were what mortals call advertisements. The diary had explained them to me just the other day.

Advertisement: a way of persuading mortals to spend money on goods or to do things that they don't want to do. Ads are not supposed to contain outright lies, but they bend the truth until it cries out, "Please stop—you're hurting me!"

As a trickster, I approve of this! Of course, Thor, the dullard, fell for them immediately.

Hmm, perhaps I should try Hammerswap? Some of my hammers are a bit old.

"You're so gullible," I said. "Ads only exist to prey upon the minds of the weak!"

Then we passed a poster advertising a new flavor of potato chips.

ALL-NEW FLAVOR
VINEGAR AND ANCHOVY
FEEL LESS ALONE!
CHIPS ARE YOUR FRIENDS!

OK, so perhaps not all ads are cons.

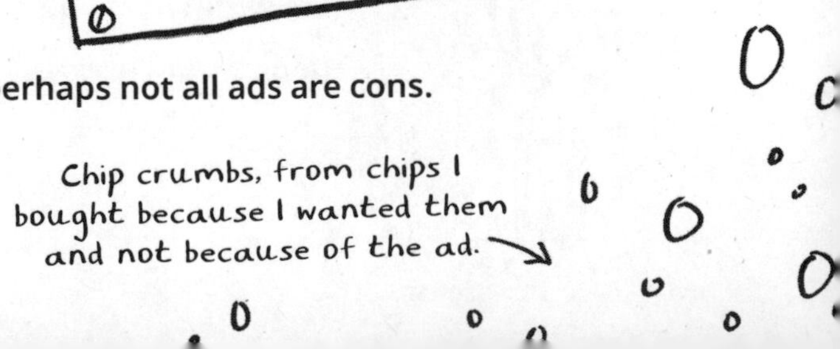
Chip crumbs, from chips I bought because I wanted them and not because of the ad.

Day Three

Wednesday

LOKI VIRTUE SCORE OR LVS:

−50

Points deducted for trying to force friendship on Sarah and destroying Valerie's drawing

Liar.
No, sweetie. I'm an actor.

In drama, we did something called improvisation. This is the best thing ever! It means making up lies on the spot and getting congratulated for it by the teacher! My entire life has led up to this moment!

We worked in pairs, but unfortunately the teacher put me with Thor, who does not understand acting.

I'm a very powerful King and you are my servant.
You're not a King. Odin's the King of the gods.
It's called acting!
Hmmmm. So I should ACT?
SIGH
Yes! Servant, fetch me a tiger.
OK.
I will take the ACTION you suggest!

I chased after him; otherwise his shattering literal-mindedness would have resulted in the local zoo losing its main attraction. Either that, or Jean the tiger would have a very angry god in her belly . . .

When I dragged him back to the drama room, I explained loudly that Thomas had had to urinate and since he was too stupid to find his way to the restroom without getting lost, I'd gone to help him. That won me a dead arm from the fist of Thor.

At the end of the lesson, as the class was filing out, the teacher went first . . .

It was hilarious. At least, it was hilarious until she got to her feet and pointed at me.

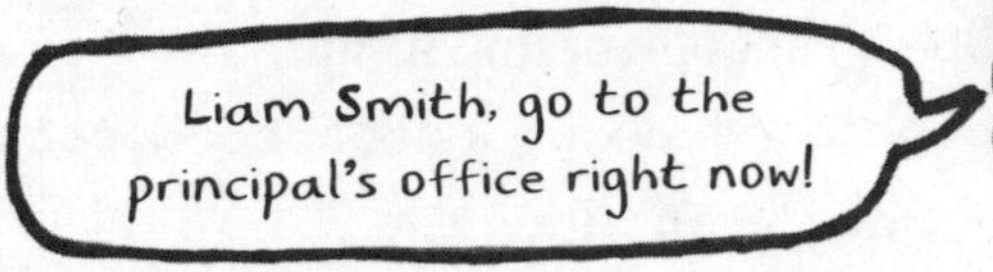
Liam Smith, go to the principal's office right now!

"But it wasn't me!" I said. And it wasn't!

Truth detected. How novel! !

"Well, you and Thomas were the only ones to leave the classroom during the lesson . . . Are you trying to tell me it was Thomas?"

Even I could not imagine Thor would—or could—have done such a hilarious thing.

"I will happily go to the principal. Although I did not do this thing, I glory that it happened!" I said, and skipped off down the corridor to face my pointless punishment. Having faced an eternity of snakes, a few stern words from an irrelevant mortal did not scare me!

As I left, Sarah scowled at me. She clearly hates fun.

I *am* intrigued to know who pulled the prank, mind you. Being the god of mischief, I consider pranks to be an act of worship to me.

! Not everything is about you.

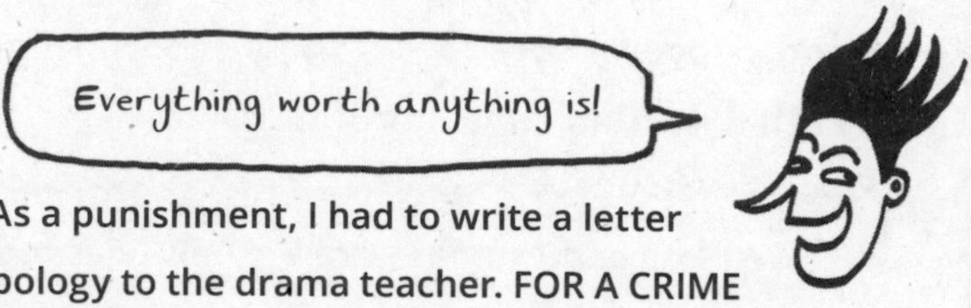
Everything worth anything is!

As a punishment, I had to write a letter of apology to the drama teacher. FOR A CRIME I DID NOT COMMIT! During my sacred lunch break! The injustice!

Then, in math, we learned about a very large number called a googolplex. How do mathematicians get up in the morning and pretend to be serious adults when they spout such idiotic-sounding words?

On a totally unrelated note—which is absolutely not the reason that I find math a silly waste of time—I only got 7/10 on the arithmetic test while stuck-up Sarah got 9/10 and Valerie got 10/10. I believe either mortal math is fundamentally misguided or Mrs. Williams marked the tests in the dark. Though she did get Thor's score correct at least (2/10). In comparison to that nincompoop, my parents' night report is going to be *glowing*. OK, my math report will be. I fear my drama report will be . . . less glowing.

Dear Ms. Loach,

I am sorry that you fell on your buttocks after slipping on a skateboard but it was not my fault therefore I am not sorry.

Yours sincerely,
Liam Smith

But before I could prove my innocence, we were interrupted by a truly horrifying noise.

BEEEEEEEEEEEEEEE-OOOOOOOOOOOOOO-
BEEEEEEEEE-OOOOOOOOOOOOO

"The alarm!" Heimdall cried.

"Yes, it is alarming," I said, covering my poor mortal ears.

BEEEEEEEEEEEEEEE-OOOOOOOOOOOOOO-
BEEEEEEEEE-OOOOOOOOOOOOO

Heimdall didn't reply but grabbed his favorite sword from the umbrella stand and rushed to the back door. He pulled it open.

"No thieves there. They must be upstairs!"

I saw no point in running upstairs. If there were thieves—or even giants—in the house, Thor and Heimdall would get *far* more pleasure out of beating them up than I would. Naturally, my actions were motivated by pure, selfless goodness and definitely not because I was afraid for my fragile mortal body with its twiglike limbs . . .

What's that I smell? Burning? I believe it may be your pants. Are they on fire, by any chance? !

Is it just me or is this diary starting to get sassy?

You're clearly a bad influence, Loki. !

BEEEEEEEEEE-OOOOOOOOOOO-
BEEEEEEEEE-OOOOOOOOOOOOOO

The noise stopped.

"Can't believe I got Mjolnir out for nothing. None of your kin up there, half-giant," Thor growled at me, as though the lack of giants was somehow my fault!

"My kin? You're half giant, too, remember!" I pointed out.

(Not a lie. His mother is a giant, and this is a sore topic for the god of farts-and-beating-up-giants-with-hammers.)

"Come over here and say that!" said Thor, shaking his hammer at me.

"I'm fine over here," I said.

"Stop it, children," said Hyrrokkin. "Or we'll send you to bed without any dinner."

"If Heimdall's cooking, then that's hardly a sacrifice," I sniffed.

"It's takeout night," said Hyrrokkin.

And so there was instant peace.

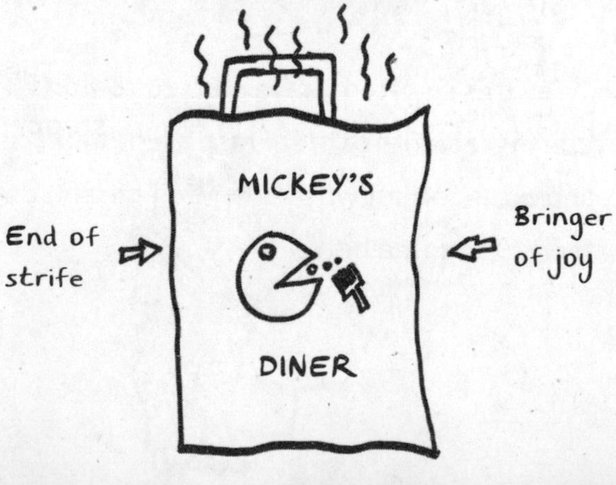

Day Four

Thursday

LOKI VIRTUE SCORE OR LVS:

-100

Points lost for teasing Thor about his mother

At breakfast, Heimdall gave me one of his lectures about being good.

blah
blah
blah
discipline
blah
blah
blah
blah
blah
blah
blah
blah
blah
blah
blah
do as I say . . .

He does this so often I have started to think of it as one of the ingredients of breakfast itself: milk, cereal, toast, and a rant about why I am a bad person and how I need to become better.

"I trust your teachers will say good things tonight at parents' night?" he said when he'd finished.

"Indeed! You should pack sandwiches and a flask containing a hot beverage, because my teachers' praise will be lengthy," I said.

I can't believe they don't have faith in my incredible intellect. Rude.

"We will walk to school as a family this morning," announced Heimdall. "My parenting books say that I need to model healthy behavior for my sons."

I grumbled, but there was nothing I could do when Heimdall had an idea in his mind. Hyrrokkin and Thor chattered together of past battles while Heimdall walked at my side in surly silence. Just as we got to the gate . . .

A tiny part of me liked being called son. Of course, that part was very silly and I wasn't listening to it.

In that moment, I realized that New Girl Sarah was watching. It was a shame that there were no earthquakes in our part of the mortal realm, for I wished very much for the ground to swallow up this witness to Heimdall rubbing disgusting spit on my face.

School was its usual dreary round of eternal nonsense. Time passed as slowly as the creep of a glacier across the frozen ground of Jotunheim. Finally, evening arrived, as did the babysitter.

Babysitter: a stranger who is entrusted with the care of mortal young for an evening. In spite of the name, they do not sit on babies, although they do tend to spend most of the evening in a seated position, either in front of the television, or playing on their phone, or both at once.

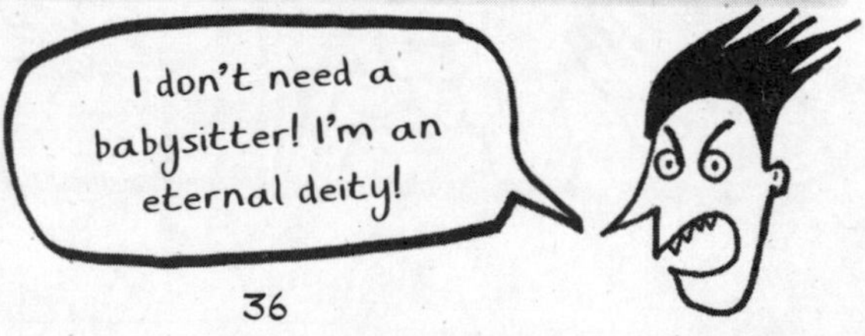

I don't need a babysitter! I'm an eternal deity!

On the plus side, Heimdall had arranged with Valerie's moms that the babysitter would come and stay with all three of us after school, so at least I had an evening with Valerie to look forward to. As soon as Valerie arrived, the babysitter switched on the television to something called a reality TV show.

Reality television: a form of entertainment that bears little resemblance to reality, in which a group of mortals often have to compete for a measly prize by performing humiliating tasks.

It seems that mortals are not so different from the gods after all—the gods of Asgard are always engaging in wholly pointless competitions. Remind me to tell you about the time Thor tried to drink the entire sea. (Long story. Involves giants, as most Thor stories do.)

I suggested a game to Valerie and Thor that I had invented recently.

DING DUNG DITCH

A variant of the mortal game known as Ding Dong Ditch or Knock and Run. In the traditional game, the mortal child knocks on a door and runs away. In my superior version, an additional first stage is included, for further glee.

- Deposit dog feces on a neighbor's doorstep—you may source the feces from your own dog or use any dog feces left unattended in the street.
- Knock on your neighbor's door.
- When they open the door, step backward so they instinctively step forward into the dog feces.
- Run away laughing.
- Repeat at each dwelling until you are caught.
- Blame the crime on a passing dog.

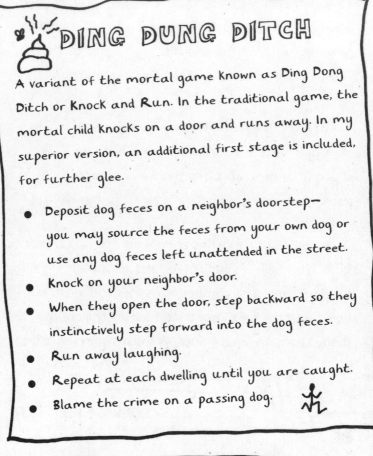

NO! We're not playing that.

Such is the way of innovation. When the astronomer Galileo discovered that the Earth orbits the sun and not the other way around, he was arrested.

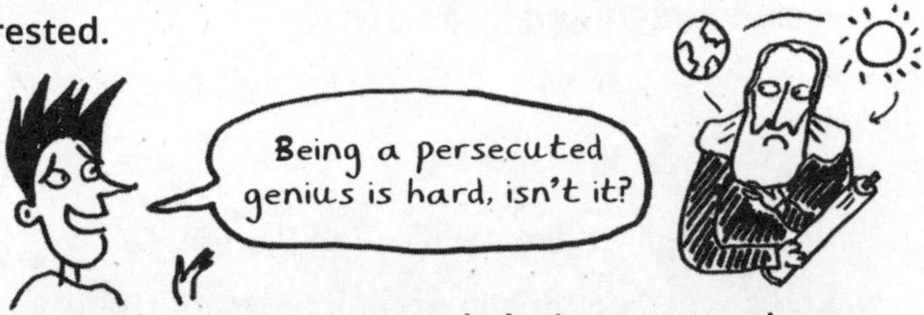

Being a persecuted genius is hard, isn't it?

Instead, Valerie suggested playing a game about owning houses. Initially I did not believe it would be fun. Why would property ownership be exciting? Even Thor agreed with me. He was dismayed by the lack of violence. But as the game went on, I started to feel a fever building inside me. I wished to own as many buildings as I could!

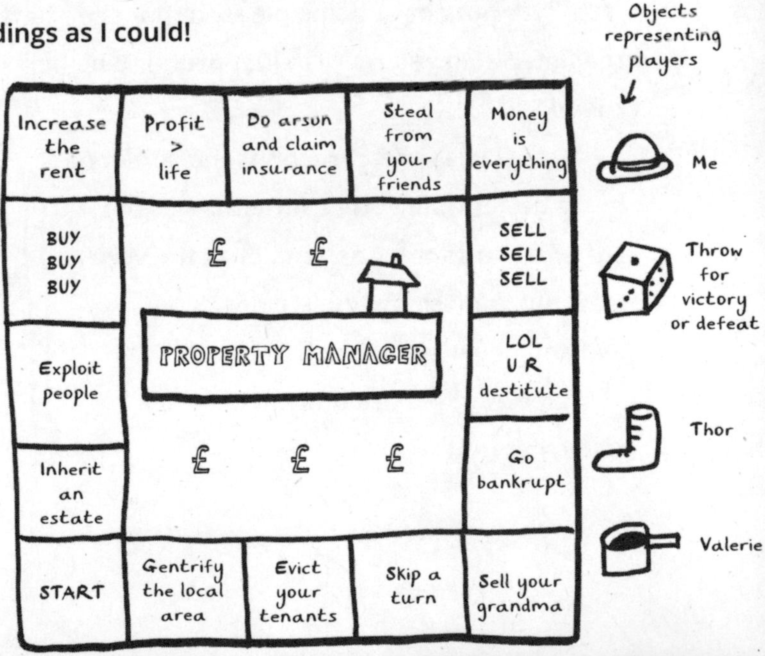

Of course, I won.

! Because you cheated. And Valerie caught you and demanded a rematch.

AHEM. Well, during the second game, Thor watched me like a hawk and Valerie talked about Georgina at great length. As she launched into yet another speech about how wonderful Georgina was at riding, I stopped her.

"I don't understand. Why do you praise her and not me? And why are you so pleased about this mortal girl being better than you at something?"

"It's not about being pleased that she's better than me," said Valerie. "I'm just proud to be her friend."

Wrong! The correct response to someone being better than you at something is to either try to sabotage them, or at the very least put something unpleasant in their bed and never speak to them again.

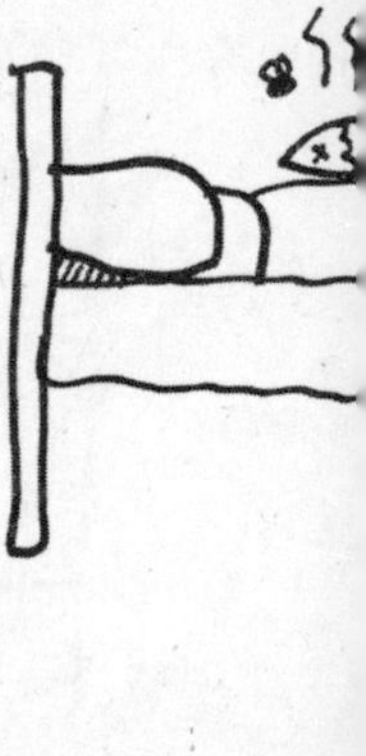

Valerie smiled dreamily. "I'm really glad I met her!"

I was not glad. I felt as though I had worms in my chest. Giant worms, with spiky teeth. Then I heard a voice . . .

You're jealous. You want Valerie all to yourself. But that's not how friendship works.
What do YOU know about friendship, O disembodied voice? Do YOU have any friends? No? Then shut up.
You're only hurting yourself by ignoring me.

Bah. My so-called conscience is even worse than the diary because it can attack at any time, such as the moment when I was *definitely* about to roll a double six.

Victory to my little metal boot!
GRRR

I thought the torture would finally end when the grown-ups returned. I was wrong.

"Valerie, you've done so well," said the mother she called Ma. She was the one who grew Valerie within her body's central regions. Just as I did when I was a horse and gave birth to Sleipnir, Odin's steed! (Believe me, growing a being inside you is deeply uncomfortable. Especially when your baby has eight legs to kick you with.)

"We're very proud of you, Valerie," said the mother she called Mom. She gave Valerie a hug.

This was not of interest to me. I was eagerly awaiting a torrent of praise about my own intellect and achievements.

But after Valerie and her moms left, Hyrrokkin and Heimdall covered Thor's report first. The audacity!

"Although your intellect is not your strongest attribute," Heimdall continued, "you always try your best. And your physical education teacher was *full* of praise."

Thor smiled. He apparently had no shame about his lack of intellect. All he cared about was having the biggest muscles and everyone loving him. So shallow and vain!

"What about me? What praise did they heap upon the name of Loki—I mean, Liam?" I asked.

NOT the expressions of fake parents who have spent the evening listening to praise about their fake son.

"Your teachers said you're clearly very capable," said Hyrrokkin, "but your behavior is disgraceful. You're rude, cruel to your fellow students—"

"But I offered the new girl a chair!" I interrupted. "That is polite and kind, not cruel!"

"Pah!" Hyrrokkin waved my objection away with her hand like the smell of a lingering fart. "That is hardly significant. Your teachers had a *long* list of misdemeanors that you have

committed. And Mrs. Williams was convinced you only offered a chair to the new girl as part of an elaborate trick."

Huh! Not fair! Judging my current behavior on my past behavior is so . . . well, judgmental!

We are very disappointed.

"Your drama teacher said how upset she was about the cruel prank you pulled on her the other day," Heimdall added.

"She really hurt her bottom falling off that skateboard," said Hyrrokkin. (Though I swear she was trying not to laugh as she said it.)

"I already told you, that wasn't me!" I complained. The injustice! I WAS INNOCENT!

"Let's say we believe you," said Hyrrokkin. "But what about the time you put pins on a teacher's chair? And the time you locked the school nurse in a closet? And the time you put plastic wrap over the principal's toilet so that his urine splashed back all over him . . . ? Need I go on?"

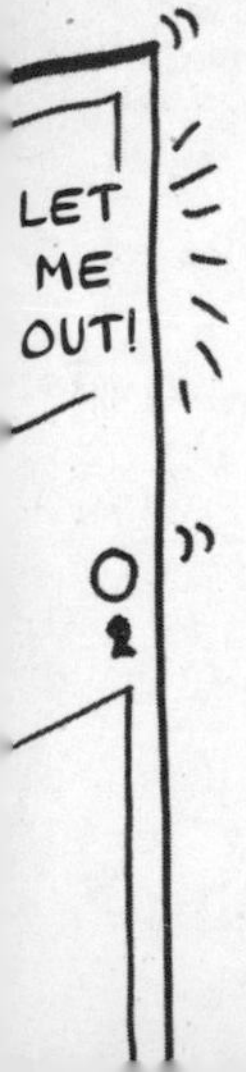
LET
ME
OUT!

OK, those *had* been my doing. I regret *nothing*, for they were all truly hilarious.

All in all, it appeared that I was *not* the teacher's pet. I wasn't even the dead mouse behind the teacher's fridge.

Even this
is too good
for you.
—Mrs. Williams

Bah! Well, school is a foolish mortal business, beneath my notice.

"What does it matter if I do well in school?" I said. "That's not what I'm on Earth to do. I'm here to protect puny mortals from Frost Giants. And you don't see any Frost Giants around right now, do you? I'm clearly doing an *excellent* job!"

"Ha, that is not your doing," said Thor. "They clearly fear *me*!"

"Also," said Heimdall, "there is another part to your quest, remember? Odin said you still have to do good deeds and write them truthfully in your diary, to show you're becoming a good person."

"My points total went up by fifty on Tuesday!" I objected.

"And how much has it gone down since?" asked Hyrrokkin. "Plus, I'm beginning to wonder if the diary feels sorry for you and has started giving you pity points."

> **!** **Little bit.**

"Let me spell it out for you," said Heimdall. "If you misbehave at school and treat your fellow mortal children and teachers with disdain, it shows you are *not* becoming a better person. You want to be worthy of Asgard, don't you?"

In that moment I didn't care about Asgard. I just wanted to be anywhere but there, sitting on an uncomfortable plastic chair, at a table covered in coffee stains, surrounded by deeply patronizing gods. Even the cold, gloomy depths of Hel or the underground realm of the dwarves would have been better! (And those dwarves get *sweaty* at their fiery forges, I can tell you.)

I expect to see improvement at school. Or . . .

Day Five

Friday

LOKI VIRTUE SCORE OR LVS:

-150

Minus points for cheating at board games

Before school, Hyrrokkin announced that we would soon be celebrating a mortal ritual known as the BIRTHDAY PARTY.

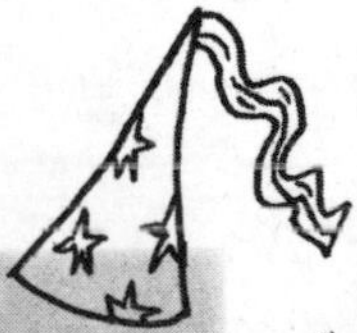

Birthday party: a time when mortals gather with friends and family to celebrate the person whose birthday it is as well as the fact that they are not yet dead. For a mortal, still being alive is quite an achievement, as they are so fragile and short-lived. There is usually cake.

As gods, we don't make a big fuss about birthdays, since we have so many of them, but Hyrrokkin thought Thor deserved celebrating and decreed that we make tomorrow Thor's birthday party. When I asked why it couldn't be mine, given we are supposed to be twins, she held up a piece of paper where she'd taken notes from parents' night and told me that people who left rotting fish in their teachers' desks did not deserve treats.

"Thor, meanwhile, proved himself worthy of celebration." She flipped over the paper. "We shall say this is a belated party because you gave Thor food poisoning on your actual shared birthday."

I can't believe they are making up foul lies about me! (I mean, I *did* give Thor food poisoning once, but it wasn't on his birthday.) And Thor was getting a party for merely *trying*. Trying is nothing. Victory is all!

"I'm going to get you for this unfairness," I spat at Thor.

But Thor was too thrilled about the party to bother with my threats. "Will there be fighting?"

"No fighting," said Heimdall.

Thor's face fell. "What about feasting?"

"We'll get you a cake," offered Hyrrokkin.

"And you can invite all your friends," said Heimdall, patting Thor on the back.

"Excellent," said Thor. "I have MANY friends. I will invite all my friends from the sports team, and all my friends from my class, and all my friends from . . ."

I shall invite
Rashmi
and James
and Jamal
and Ben
and Kamala
and Nyla
and Mohammed
and Luka
and Jamie
and Evie
and Riley
and Malcom
and Joshua
and Ming
and

Thor continued for at least five minutes listing all his friends. I'm surprised he can count that high.

Hyrrokkin looked at me and her face softened a little. "You can invite your friends, too, Loki."

"I shall," I said. "I shall invite my many friends."

"Who?" asked Thor.

"I am a very mysterious god with a rich and varied social life, so you wouldn't know them all," I sniffed. "It will be a surprise."

...

So . . . I have a day to make some new friends.

Thor texted all his friends on the way to school, and by the time we got there he already had roughly 90,000 people on the guest list. I don't know how they'll all fit into our pathetic mortal house. Especially the muscular, sports-playing ones.

I, meanwhile, had managed to invite zero friends. The reason is because I'm a Good God™ now and texting while walking is antisocial and dangerous.

! **Lie detected. That was not the reason.**

Well, at least I had one existing friend to count on.

I felt a shriek of pure rage building within me. But then I had an idea.

"Bring her along!" I said. "My fake parents said I could invite as many friends as I like."

Valerie gave me a perplexed look. "But Georgina isn't your friend—you haven't even met yet."

"I am a god," I sniffed. "I am above mere details of linear time. Just bring her." Then I tried a "Please?"

"I'm so glad you want to meet her!" said Valerie. "I just know you two are going to be great friends."

She's SOOOO amazing.
I'm SOOOO tired of hearing about her.

Then she looked puzzled. "Wait. Aren't you supposed to be twins? Why is the birthday party only for Thor?"

"Apparently I'm being punished for my bad school report," I said. But the true punishment would come if Thor ended up with more guests than I!

Operation Get More Friends went into overdrive as soon as I reached the classroom. Before the English lesson began, I wandered over to New Girl Sarah. She might have been too shy to accept my offers of friendship thus far, but today I wasn't letting her insecurities get in the way of our beautiful, blossoming relationship!

"There's an amazing party tomorrow," I said. "All the popular people are invited."

"Where's the party?" she asked. She sounded cold and mean and a little bit angry with me, the *classic* signs of shyness. Mortals are so easy to read.

"At my house!" I said. "I'm the brother of the birthday boy, and I'm allowed to invite anyone I like."

My trap was laid. Would she fall in?

Then I saw a glint of excitement in her eye, as though she was suddenly understanding that this was a great gift and I was, in fact, her generous social savior.

Excellent. *Snap!* went the trap.

I mean, "Yay, a new friend."

That's three on Loki's friend slate.

In music and French, I persuaded four more people to come as my guests by promising to show them Hyrrokkin's snakes.

By the end of the day, my guest list was a very respectable ten. My powers of persuasion have not dimmed in spite of this pathetic mortal form! Thor doesn't need to know that three of my "friends" will be coming because I threatened to put slimy things in their hair if they didn't. (I was running out of ideas by the end of the day, and threats are just so simple and elegant, don't you think?)

! **No.**

That was a rhetorical question and you know it!

Day Six

Saturday

LOKI VIRTUE SCORE OR LVS:

-200

Points lost for using threats and lies and bribery to trick people into coming to the party

No self-respecting feast in Asgard would begin until the sun set, but mortal children are made of puny stuff, so the party began in the early afternoon.

Heimdall had done a lot of research and adorned the living room with a giant sign.

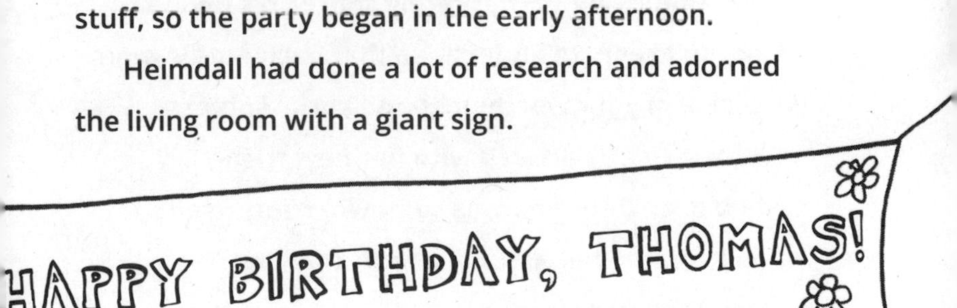

Pointless. All the guests know that it is a birthday party and whose birthday it is.

Thor's friend Sportsboy One arrived first.

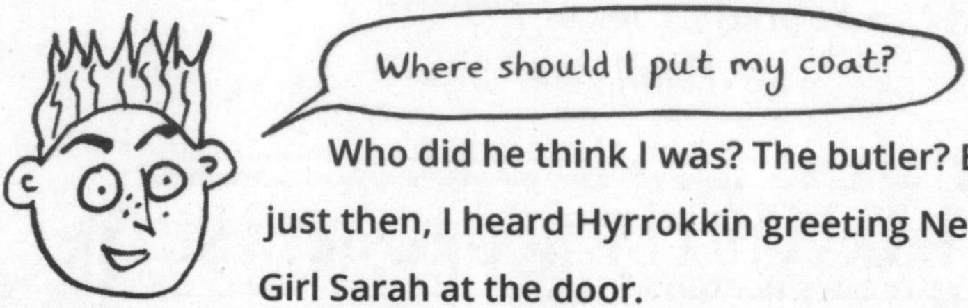
Where should I put my coat?

Who did he think I was? The butler? But just then, I heard Hyrrokkin greeting New Girl Sarah at the door.

"Figure it out yourself," I said, pushing past him. "I must welcome my very good friend Sarah!"

As each of my other guests arrived, I greeted them loudly and within Thor's hearing.

Annoyingly, Thor was too busy speaking to his own friends to notice, so I took lots of photos on my phone and posted them, tagging Thor, so he'd know of my popularity when he next checked his phone. (Annoyingly, Thor rarely checks his phone. He doesn't seem to understand that each notification is a signal of your worthiness and social success.)

When Valerie arrived with her new friend, I rushed over. Georgina was somewhat surprised when I greeted her as I would a dear friend. In case Thor was looking.

Darling!
Er . . . hi?

She was, as Valerie had said, very pretty. But any dullard can be pretty. Look at Thor.

"Thank you for inviting me, Liam," Georgina said. Then she held out a box. "I brought a present for your brother. Where should I put it?"

"His room's upstairs," I said, waving her away. I don't know why Valerie thought she was so amazing. She'd already been in my presence for at least thirty seconds and had yet to make even one devastatingly witty comment!

"Are you OK?" asked Valerie while Georgina was upstairs. "Or are you upset because all the people you invited are hanging out with"—she leaned in and whispered—"Thor?"

It was true. Every single person I had invited apart from Valerie and Georgina (who wasn't actually in the room) were giving Thor The Look.

Even Sarah, the new girl, was hanging off his every word as he told tales of his sporting prowess.

Thankfully, Georgina returned, saving me from having to answer.

"What should we do now?" she said, casually putting an arm around Valerie's shoulders.

I had a few thoughts of things I would like to happen next . . .

But none of them were in my control.

"Let's eat," Valerie suggested.

At mortal children's parties, it is apparently the custom to eat food that mortal parents do not allow their spawn to consume at any other time.

Pig intestines surrounded by bread matter
I do not know why it is this color but it looks like a crime against nature.
Sugar on top of some more sugar

Valerie and Georgina demolished a plate of cookies and talked about horses. I wasn't hungry but I put a cookie in my pocket because it felt a bit like stealing. I miss stealing, now that I'm a Good God™.

The party was not going the way I had planned. None of my new friends were paying any attention to me, Valerie was only paying attention to Georgina, and the birthday rituals were very unpleasant. They involved . . .

Out-of-tune singing
A game where you win prizes for stopping dancing
But my dancing is EXCELLENT. Why would I stop?
Thor spitting on a burning cake

We then had to *eat* the cake covered in Thor-spit. Mortals are so disgusting. Perhaps that's why Thor fits in so well here?

I went to bed feeling glad it was all over, but I had horrible dreams.

Day Seven

Sunday

LOKI VIRTUE SCORE OR LVS:

-250

Points lost for not buying Thor a birthday present

Bah! Loki does not buy fake birthday presents for fake brothers!

Then it's not surprising real Loki loses real points then, is it?

!

Today was a disaster. No, it was a tragedy.

I immediately knew that the day would not go well when a roar shook the house.

IT IS GONE!
NOOOOO!
What's wrong?
Excited pee
THUMP
THUMP
AHHH!
What's gone?
In Thor's room . . .
Thor's hammers
MISSING

"My hammer Mjolnir!" Thor cried. "I went to polish it and it was GONE!"

"Where did you last see it?" I asked.

"I meant: When?" I said.

"It was there before the party," said Thor.

Heimdall looked thoughtful. "It wasn't there last night when I came to turn your lights out. I thought you must have stowed it away for safekeeping while we had guests."

"It's been *stolen*." Thor turned to me and glared.

Heimdall and Hyrrokkin both turned to me, too. Even Fido glared at me.

"What? I didn't take your stupid hammer! I got you that hammer as a present in the first place. Why would I steal it?" (Long story. It involves a ship that can fit in your pocket. I'll tell you when I'm not being falsely accused of crimes against Thor.)

Thor wasn't listening—he looked as though he was about to pound me into a Loki-flavored paste.

"No!" Heimdall stepped in between us. "Let us handle this calmly."

"When has Thor ever handled anything calmly? There's a thunderstorm every time he stubs his toe," I pointed out.

"You little—" began Thor.

But Heimdall interrupted. "We can simply summon Odin," he said. "With his mighty powers, he can uncover the truth!"

I wanted to object. *I* knew I was not guilty. We didn't need Poo-Poo Head Odin to tell us that.

! His proper title is ALLFATHER, Loki.

I was too slow. Heimdall was already speaking the magic words that would summon He-Who-Bosses-Everyone-Around-and-Has-a-Stupid-Beard:

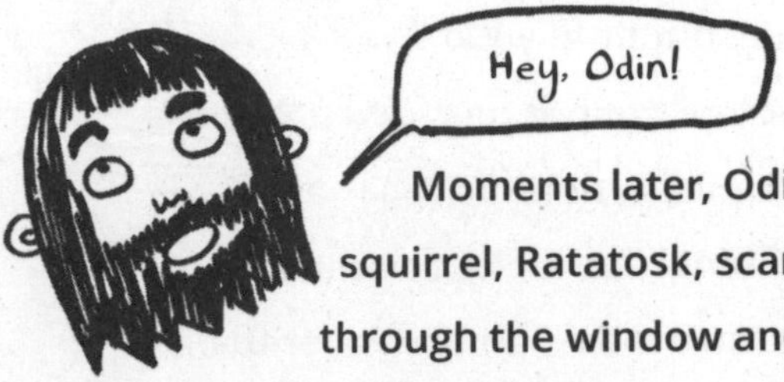

Moments later, Odin's messenger squirrel, Ratatosk, scampered in through the window and held up a scroll.

—THIS IS AN AUTOMATIC OUT-OF-ASGARD REPLY—

Odin isn't home right now. He is on a secret quest for wisdom. He will get back to you on his return—that is, in a little under one month according to the mortal calendar, a full feast cycle according to the time of Asgard, or Three Beards according to Dwarven Standard Time. He will manifest in your presence on his return.

Sent on behalf of: ODIN, Allfather of the gods of Asgard, Wisest of the Wise.

"Well, we don't need Odin anyway," I said as the squirrel scampered away. "I'm innocent!"

"Prove it," said Heimdall.

"No thanks. That sounds like hard work. I'm Loki, god of mischief, not god of drudgery! *You* prove I did it. Or, if we're flinging around accusations, I accuse the Frost Giants!"

Heimdall shook his head. "Can't be Frost Giants. No one broke in overnight. My alarm didn't go off."

"And I definitely didn't invite any Frost Giants to the party," added Thor.

Hyrrokkin was looking more closely at the space where Thor's hammer should be. She reached for something and plucked it up.

I couldn't believe this was happening. "There's lots of reasons why my hair might be there! Maybe I brushed my hair in Thor's room?"

"You never brush your hair," Hyrrokkin pointed out.

"I combed it once two weeks ago!" I objected.

"Why are we wasting time? It's clearly him!" said Thor. "Loki swore vengeance upon me for my good report and my birthday party."

"Ah," I said. "You heard that?"

"We all heard it," said Hyrrokkin.

"Tell us where you put the hammer, Loki," growled Heimdall. "It better be somewhere safe!"

This was a new situation for me. Usually when the gods of Asgard accuse me of a crime, they are correct. This time, as with the drama teacher, the gods were accusing me of a crime I didn't commit.

And those gods were VERY ANGRY.

Which is when I realized that I *could* prove that I was innocent. And I didn't need Odin's help.

I ran upstairs, grabbed this diary, and wrote:

Then I ran downstairs again, giving the diary time to get all annoyed about me writing a lie in the book and write "Lie detected" next to my statement. As soon as I got back to the others, I opened the pages expecting to see proof of my innocence. Except, instead of "I STOLE THE HAMMER" followed by "Lie detected," the book now read:

I STOLE THE HAMMER.

!

NICE TRY, LOKI.

We've talked about this. I am not your personal soothsayer, nor am I here to get you out of trouble.

"Why are you waving your book around, Loki?" asked Hyrrokkin.

I sighed deeply. "Never mind, it's nothing."

But this would not defeat me! I would have victory! I would find the real culprit and point at them, saying, "That stinky poo-poo head did the deed, not I! For I am as innocent as a very sweet-smelling baby bird!"

I turned to face the others and swore an oath.

I began Project Clear Loki's Name immediately.

First, I searched Thor's room in case he'd left his hammer somewhere like the laundry basket.

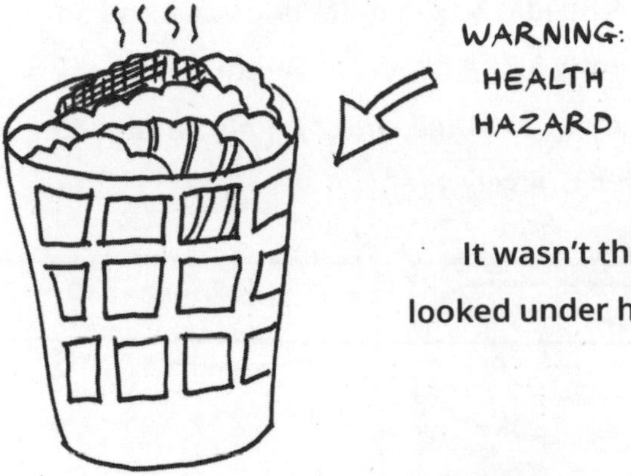

It wasn't there. Then I looked under his bed . . .

and in the bathroom . . .

and in the drawer in the kitchen where Hyrrokkin keeps the tools with which she repairs our decaying hovel.

But it was nowhere.

So, someone clearly took it. But who?

In Asgard, crimes are reported to Odin, who then asks Mimir's head who did it. (Mimir is a wise god who is currently just a head—long story involving a war, an annoying hostage, and a highly flammable woman called Gullveig.)

But since I couldn't get hold of Odin at the moment, I tried Midgard's answer to Mimir: the internet.

Search HOW DO YOU SOLVE A CRIME?

It turned out that in the mortal realm, crimes are usually solved by people called police.

Police, the: mortals who are allowed to lock other mortals away and generally punish them.

Huh, so basically they're a bunch of Odins. I won't be calling THEM. I don't trust anyone who can throw you in prison after my experience in Odin's cells. Still, I don't like to rely too much on this diary's definitions, so I did some research of my own. Apparently there are a number of types of police, including . . .

Police officers: these wear matching outfits so you can see them coming.

Traffic police: I don't have a car so I don't care about them.

Detectives: police who get all the credit for solving crimes AND wear normal clothes so you can't spot them easily, which makes me nervous.

However, according to the internet, some of the best detectives don't work for the police. True, they're often made up by writers, but I am the god of lies—the idea that something is made up does not put me off!

One such detective, a Miss Marple, solves crimes purely by being nosy, and another, called Sherlock Holmes, outwits criminal minds by being a genius. (That was very encouraging to read. I, too, am a genius so this should be easy!)

The internet also told me that you need to know THREE THINGS in order to solve a crime. (Admittedly, it told me that after I'd spent an hour reading about how to plan the perfect murder. If the universe wanted to make me focus on the task at hand, it shouldn't make the internet so full of wonders!)

THINGS YOU NEED TO KNOW IN ORDER TO SOLVE A CRIME:

Motive: Does the suspect have a reason to commit the crime (for example, will they inherit money after their aunt dies under "mysterious circumstances")?

Means: Does the suspect have the equipment or tools to do the crime (such as a murder weapon, or enough money to pay an assassin)?

Opportunity: Was the suspect in the right place at the right time to commit the crime?

After doing some more research, I decided it was time to call Valerie. Not because I needed help and couldn't figure out what to do next, but because every detective needs a slightly-less-intelligent-but-still-very-useful sidekick. A Watson to my Holmes.

Thank you for noticing that clue, my dear Valerie. I will now solve the crime with my genius and patronize you while I explain the solution.

So I called Valerie and told her what had happened.

She started sidekicking immediately. “Right. The only people who had the opportunity to steal the hammer were the ones who went upstairs that evening,” she said.

I hadn’t noticed who went upstairs because I am above caring about the comings and goings of fools. But Valerie had. This is why sidekicks are important.

“That leaves you; Georgina; that new girl, Sarah; Sportsboy One; Thor; Heimdall; and Hyrrokkin.”

“So—” I began.

But she cut me off. BAD SIDEKICK!

“Now that you have a list of suspects,” she went on, “you need to figure out who had the means to commit the crime—which is all of you, because taking a hammer and hiding it isn’t hard . . . So really it’s all down to who had a motive.”

Enough was enough. I had to put my foot down and make it clear who was the sidekick and who was the detective.

"I shall spend the evening pondering who might have a motive," I said in my most thoughtful and genius-filled voice.

"And I shall spend the evening doing a new horse drawing for Georgina," said Valerie. "The old one got trampled," she added sadly. "It fell off my desk somehow . . ."

"Very drafty in that classroom," I said, not really paying attention. My mind was whirring. I didn't like this new Georgina obsession one little bit. My best friend was being stolen right from under my nose. Just like Thor's hammer, only larger and more Valerie-shaped!

As a distraction, I threw myself into solving the theft of Thor's hammer.

WHO DUNNIT?

From watching a few hours of television detective shows, I learned that boards with string on them help you solve crime. I'm not sure how the string helps, but it clearly works because TV detectives solve every crime in under an hour!

THE SUSPECTS

SPORTSBOY ONE

Thor's sportsball teammate. Had the opportunity since he went upstairs to leave his coat in Thor's room. (Thor advised him to do this because the coat was expensive and his "brother" was not "trustworthy.") RUDE!

GEORGINA

Valerie's horse friend (and attempted friend thief). Had the opportunity since she went upstairs to put Thor's present in his room.

SARAH

New girl, shy and lacking in self-confidence. Went upstairs to use the bathroom while the downstairs one was busy with Thor's flatulent bottom.

So, who dunnit? I shall sleep on this problem and no doubt dream a genius solution. All I know is that the guilty must be punished!

! **You didn't like the guilty being punished when it was you who was guilty.**

That's different! If I was being punished, that would be very unpleasant for ME. Also, I'm not talking to you. You didn't help me when I needed you!

! **You ARE talking to me. Technically every word you write in these pages is you talking to me.**

I HATE YOU! I HOPE YOU GET EATEN BY BOOKWORMS!

Day Eight

Monday

LOKI VIRTUE SCORE OR LVS:

-350

Points lost for threatening this diary with bookworms

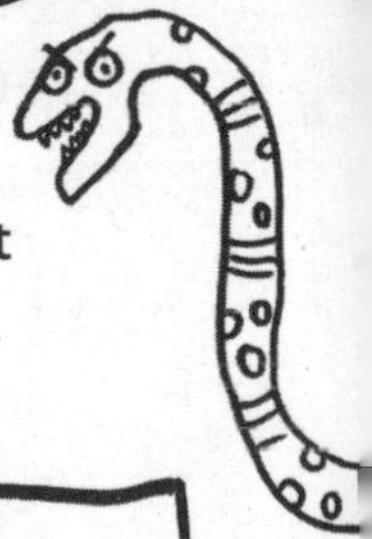

In art class, Valerie wrote out the suspect list.

I thought it looked a bit too short, so I padded it out with some more possibilities.

- A giant disguised as a beetle that crawled into Thor's room. No, that doesn't work. A beetle wouldn't be able to carry Mjolnir. X
- An evil teleporting clone of Valerie created by a magic spell. (Actually, I quite liked that theory. Valerie was less excited.) X

- The husband. (Thor doesn't have a husband, but from what Valerie says about detective stories, it's usually the husband. Thor *nearly* had a husband once. Long story. I'll tell you about it when my name is no longer under a cloud of suspicion.)

Still, the only serious contenders remaining were Sportsboy One, Georgina, and New Girl Sarah.

At that point, the teacher realized we were writing lists instead of drawing a bowl of fruit, so we had to stop solving a heinous crime and draw a "still life" instead.

RIP
Still life? This fruit is very clearly dead!

As I drew, I watched the two suspects in our class, trying to decide who had the greater motive to steal Thor's hammer. Sportsboy One was laughing and joking with Thor, as though they were the best of friends.

New Girl Sarah was giving Thor The Look, so why would she steal his hammer? Unless she was annoyed that *he* didn't invite her to the party himself? Spurned love can indeed be a motive for crime. Not that I'd know. I've never been spurned. Everyone loves Loki.

Lie detected. In fact, that should be LIE, because it's such an enormous piece of untruth-telling. **!**

You don't have to be quite so sure about that, dearest Diary . . .

At break, Valerie went over to talk to Georgina and said she'd be back in a second. But as the seconds ticked by, she proved herself a *great big liar.* See, Diary, it's not only me who lies!

Just then I spotted Sportsboy One sitting alone on the playground after banging his knee playing sportsball. I swooped in.

“What a shame about your leg,” I said, sitting down beside him. (If you are sympathetic to people, they’re more likely to tell you things. It’s a classic trickster move.)

Why do you care?
I hate to see a fellow human being in pain.

“You’re so weird,” said Sportsboy One.

“Says the person who’s best friends with my brother, Thomas,” I said, casually dropping Thor into the conversation.

“What?” said Sportsboy One, with a look of withering scorn. “Just because we’re on the same team doesn’t mean Thomas is my friend. I came to his birthday party to get out of helping my dad with the housework.”

Interesting. So he merely appears to be a good friend of Thor. Could this be our prime suspect? Sportsboy One soon left me to rejoin the game, and I watched him, looking for clues.

The game went like this:

A flash of genius entered my brilliant brain. What if Sportsboy One dislikes Thor because Thor is better at sportsball? It pains me to admit it, but Thor is always the best at every physical pursuit. And envy is a reason for which mortals have committed crimes throughout history.

! **Correction: I usually let visual inaccuracies slide, but I MUST complain that Vikings did not wear horned helmets. You just like to draw them to mess with people. Also because your true form has horns and you are incredibly self-centered.**

Vikings? Some might call them Vikings, I suppose. But I just call them "my fans." Anyway, you're interrupting my moment of triumph! The crime was solved! Once the inane nonsense of sportsball was over, I sidled up to Thor. "If I was to tell you I know who took your hammer, what would you say?"

"I'd say, give me back my hammer," he growled.

I tried again. “You have a secret enemy who might be plotting against you.”

“You’re not my secret enemy, Loki. You’re pretty public about it.”

“No, not me, you oaf,” I said. “Your secret enemy is . . .”

Now, as a masterful storyteller, I know that it’s very important to leave long dramatic pauses when you’re about to reveal something.

But Thor scoffed. "Oh, you mean Ben of the Inferior Ball Skills? He's jealous of my skills, certainly. But he does not know I am a god, so why would he steal my hammer?"

Irritating. Thor had thought of something that I had not. That was against the laws of nature!

To add insult to injury, Thor went on to make more good points.

"Anyway," he said, "it's not like he knows you're a trickster god who's always behind every crime. To Ben, you are just my annoying puny brother. So why would he frame you?"

Mortifyingly, he was right. How had that fact escaped my genius? But it was true. Sportsboy One might have had the *opportunity* to commit the crime, but his motive was looking flimsier than the rainbow bridge in the prophecy of Ragnarok! (Long prophecy. It involves the rainbow bridge, an army of giants, and the end of the world. I'll tell you everything—once it's actually happened.)

Whoever stole the hammer had to have a motive for taking the hammer *and* to frame me for doing so.

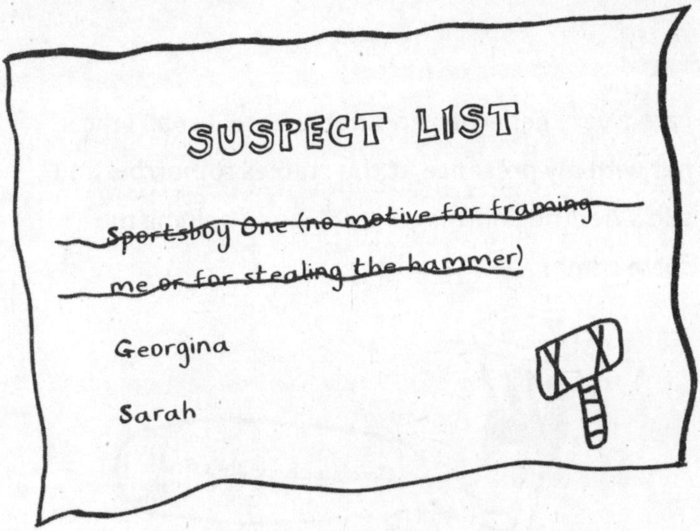
SUSPECT LIST
Sportsboy One (no motive for framing me or for stealing the hammer)
Georgina
Sarah

It was time to call upon my trusty sidekick. Except Valerie was busy all afternoon, so I messaged her after school.

Valerie, I need to talk to you about Sarah and Georgina's possible motives to steal Thor's hammer and frame me.

Sorry, can't chat now, I have to pack my riding stuff because I'm going to the stables first thing in the morning.

Honestly, I'm starting to think she's as bad at being a sidekick as Heimdall is at personal grooming. But

I am a very generous and noble hero. I shall grace her with my presence at the stables tomorrow and allow her the enormous privilege of helping me solve crimes.

Day Nine

Tuesday

LOKI VIRTUE SCORE OR LVS:

-350

Holding steady but no progress

Luckily, I know where the stables are. In fact, their location is burned into my bottom's memory because they're next to where the rainbow bridge dumped me when I first fell from Asgard.

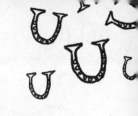

I arrived before Valerie, so, while I waited, I petted the horses. Unlike some people, the horses understood that I was very important and special and right in all things.

OK, they understood that I had sugar cubes. But the effect was the same.

As the horse licked the remaining sugar from my fingers, I saw one of the mortal staff members cutting mistletoe from a tree, complaining loudly about it looking untidy. Untidy? There was literal *horse dung* upon the ground everywhere! I'd start with the poop before fixing the plants if I were them.

Also, mistletoe is a key ingredient in many spells. And these mortals were throwing it away as though it was rubbish! The fools!

Valerie arrived and I complained about this folly, but she rolled her eyes. "Mistletoe is poisonous to horses—of *course* they have to get rid of it! I thought you said you knew all about horses?"

"I do! I *was* a horse, remember?"

"How could I forget? You're always going on about it!" said Valerie.

I snorted. "Well, when I was a horse, I was too smart to eat poisonous magical plants!"

"Fine. But . . . why are you here?"

"To discuss the case of the missing hammer, of course!" Honestly, she was being a little dense.

But I didn't invite you.
And I came anyway!
Aren't you lucky?!

Valerie let out the smallest of sighs. She was clearly harboring some secret sadness. I would soon distract her from that.

"OK, we can talk about your case," she said. "But you need to help me while we talk."

I agreed and followed her. She said we were going to do something called "mucking out." I was horrified to discover that this meant shoveling horse excrement. And—if you can believe this—the mortals who own the stables get *children* to do this *for free*. What monsters! Apparently, Valerie saw no problem with this. In fact, she considers it to be a treat! Mortals are unbelievably stupid sometimes!

Just last week in history, we learned about child labor in Victorian times, and Valerie was shocked when she found out that young children had to climb up chimneys to clean them—often for no wages. How does she not realize that what she's doing is exactly the same? Or worse, because sometimes chimney sweeps did get paid!

I refused to take part in this exploitation of vulnerable children, so I watched Valerie do it instead and we talked about the stolen hammer. We started off discussing whether Georgina might have done it, but Valerie kept getting too distracted by how "amazing" and "lovely" Georgina was. I didn't want to listen to that, so I started coming up with theories about Sarah:

THEORY ONE: Sarah had mistaken Thor (aka Thomas) for her long-lost twin brother and decided to steal his hammer, thinking it was a family heirloom, and framed me in order to determine if I was truly brother to Thor (aka Thomas) or merely a kidnapper.

That sounds like a lot of nonsense. !

THEORY TWO: Sarah is a sleepwalker and she fell asleep on the pile of coats at the party and stole the hammer while she was sleepwalking. The reason she framed me was because she was dreaming of how awesome I am and her subconscious mind turned that awe into hostility!

Wait, I take it back. The first one was silly. THIS one is nonsense. !

THEORY THREE: She stole the hammer because she has a rare condition that means her body craves hammers and she framed me for the crime because she'd watched the same detective TV shows as me which say that the criminal is usually someone very close to the victim. And I sleep so close to Thor that I can hear his snores through the thin wall between our bedrooms, so you don't get much closer than that.

! Loki, are you reading these back to yourself?

Just as I was starting to get into a *very* cunning theory based on the idea that Sarah is a time traveler from the future and stealing the hammer and framing me would set off a chain of events leading to her becoming supreme leader of the world . . . disaster struck.

Georgina arrived.

"Oh, I didn't know you were coming this morning!" said Valerie, looking overjoyed.

I don't know why she was pleased. We were about to break the case wide open, and now everything was ruined! We couldn't speak frankly before this mortal!

"I'm so glad you're here, too! We can muck out together!" said Georgina. The two girls were literally leaping up and down with glee.

"Why are you so excited about moving excrement around?" I asked. When I have to pick up Fido's poop, I do not rejoice. I gag. And more importantly, why didn't Valerie welcome MY surprise visit with a mortal jumping ritual?

"Oh, hi, Liam," said Georgina. She gave me a long, thoughtful look. "It's not about the mucking-out. I just like caring for the horses and spending time with them. And my new friend Valerie, of course," she added, giving Valerie a little arm punch.

Valerie grinned from ear to ear and gave her a punch back, until suddenly they were giggling and shoving each other, and then Georgina was chasing Valerie out of the stable into the yard, shrieking with joy.

Where are you going?
hee hee hee
hee hee
hee
hee hee hee
hee
hee

Meanwhile, I was standing alone, surrounded by horse feces, collapsing under a great sense of crushing emptiness.

I wandered out into the stable yard after them, but they were in the distance, running. I had no desire to run after them, for feats of physical prowess are beneath my dignity. But as I watched them, frolicking and yelling and running, looking so happy and carefree, inspiration struck like a bolt of Thor's lightning. I felt genius flow through my puny mortal body.

I knew who stole the hammer.

GEORGINA.

Georgina was the culprit. Every part of my cunning being screamed, "WHO DUNNIT? SHE DUNNIT!"

Not EVERY part, Loki. I'm saying different.

HUSH!

I saw it all now. She'd framed me for a crime so she could steal Valerie away from me! And if she can steal a friend, why not a hammer?

Loki, I think you must be the world's worst detective. That doesn't make sense in the slightest.

OK, admittedly I wasn't sure why this mortal would *want* Thor's hammer. And she could have framed me for a more obvious human crime, such as robbing a bank.

Unless . . . she was *not human*.

Yes . . . of course. Why didn't I think of it before? She was clearly . . .

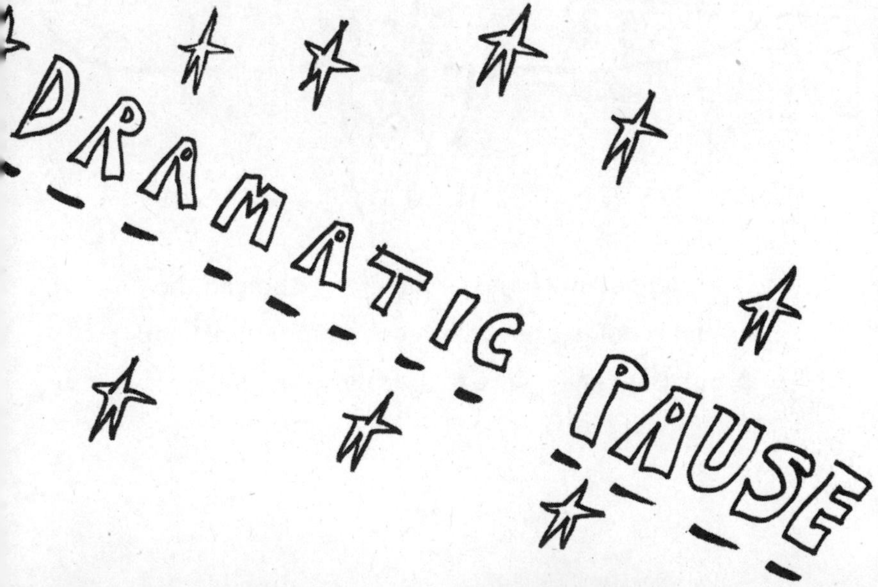

I clapped my hands in delight. I'd solved the crime! I couldn't tell Valerie my theory until I had proof. But I knew who to ask: Hyrrokkin!

After school Thor and I walked home in silence, as he's decided he isn't talking to me today. In theory, Thor's silence would be golden, but his version of not talking to me involves glaring at me until small thunderclouds form over my head, soaking me, and tiny bolts of lightning give me little electric shocks. He claims he always does this when he's angry, but I am pretty sure this is a lie given that he gets furious when his team loses at sportsball and no one at school gets electrocuted.

I waited patiently—OK, very impatiently—until after dinner when I could get Hyrrokkin alone. As she washed the plates, I asked, ever so casually, "How can you tell whether someone is a giant in disguise?"

Hyrrokkin gave me a look full of distrust. Mind you, she has resting distrust face so perhaps that wasn't personal.

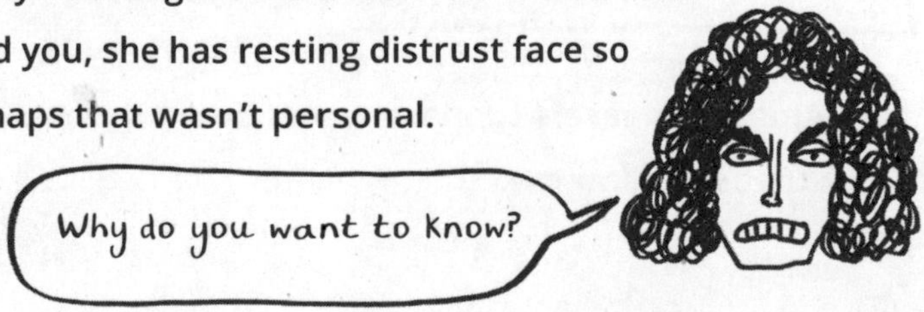

"I think the hammer thief might be a Frost Giant in disguise," I said. "After all, the Frost Giants have it in for me after the last time we crossed paths, so naturally they'd want to frame me for a crime. Plus, they would definitely want Thor's hammer, considering how often he uses it to hit Frost Giants."

I didn't tell her which "amazing" and "pretty" disguise I believed this Frost Giant to be using.

"I wish you gods wouldn't always assume it's giants," Hyrrokkin grunted as she dried her hands on a dish towel.

"Well, I wish everyone wouldn't always assume it's me," I said.

"Fair point," said Hyrrokkin. "And in this case, I suppose giants do make sense as a theory. Follow me."

We went into the living room, and she pulled down a book from the shelf. It was one of the books she'd brought with her from home (in the non-evil part of Jotunheim).

I don't know much about magic, as it was frowned upon in Asgard. Gods can be very snobby about it. The gods' own powers, of course, did not count as magic. It was only spells involving ingredients and magic words that they distrusted. Mostly because giants did them.

"Why *does* Odin hate magic so much?" I asked as Hyrrokkin placed the book back.

"Odin? He doesn't. He just made that up to stop you from learning spells and causing even more trouble," she said.

At first I was furious. But then . . . I had to respect that level of trickery.

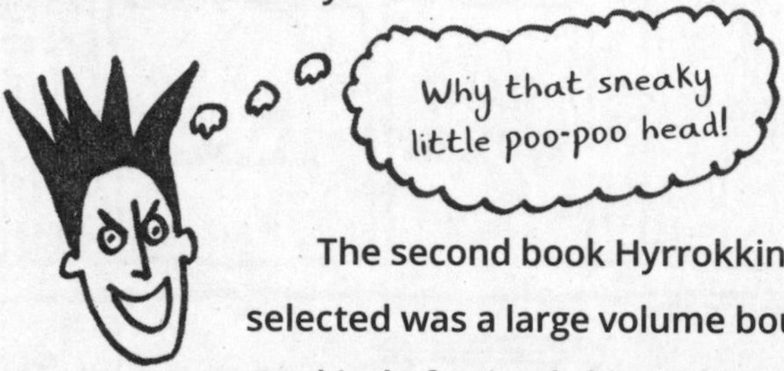
Why that sneaky little poo-poo head!

The second book Hyrrokkin selected was a large volume bound in some kind of animal skin with runes on the cover. The runes said, simply, "SPELLS." She leafed through it until she found what she was looking for.

"Ah, here. This is how to tell if a giant is really a giant. You need some of their saliva, the tears of a cat, and the bark of a dog. Mix them together and the solution will turn blue if they're a giant."

SPELLS

"How can I mix the bark of the dog with anything?" I asked.

"You shouldn't be too literal when it comes to magic," said Hyrrokkin. "It's *magic*. Just get a dog to bark while you're mixing the saliva and the tears, and you're good to go."

So all I needed to do to prove Georgina was an evil friend-stealing Frost Giant in disguise was to test her spit. Disgustingly simple!

I couldn't tell Valerie who the giant was until I had proof, but I couldn't resist showing her that I'd solved the mystery.

I have news! I have almost solved the case of Thor's missing hammer!

WOW!!!

I've decided no mortal had a motive to perform this crime. I think it must be a giant in disguise.

OMG. How do we catch them?

I'm working on it.

Valerie doesn't suspect the truth about Georgina, the pure, innocent child. She'll be so pleased and impressed when I save her from a deceitful friend-stealing giant!

! Oh, Loki. Loki, Loki, Loki.

Do you have something you want to say to me?

! Nothing you'll listen to.

Day Ten

Wednesday

LOKI VIRTUE SCORE OR LVS:

–350

I can't deduct points for plotting against Georgina as there is a theoretical possibility that she could be guilty. But just you wait . . .

I tried to test Georgina's spit at break by challenging her to a spitting contest.

"That's disgusting! No way," she said.

Oh, the cunning of giants is MIGHTY. But I will not be defeated.

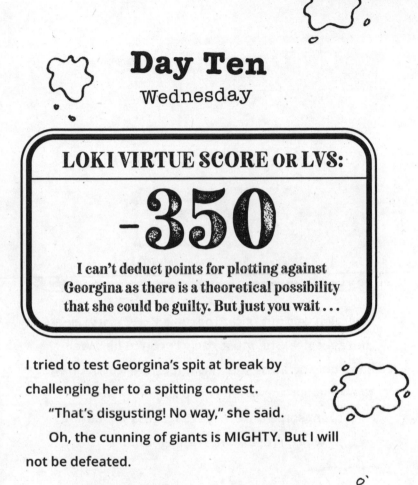

Day Eleven

Thursday

LOKI VIRTUE SCORE OR LVS:

-350

Holding steady but I'm WATCHING YOU . . .

Georgina was out "sick" today—a likely story; giants don't get sick. She must know I'm on to her! Well, she's only delaying the inevitable. I will catch up with her—and her spit—before too long!

I spent some time in language arts pondering exactly which Frost Giant she might be.

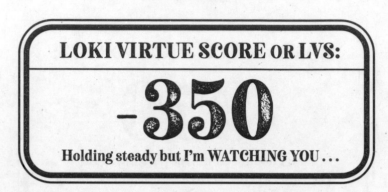

Who IS she underneath that irritating mortal exterior?

Hmmm. Maybe not.

Whichever one she is, I'll prove that Georgina is a giant for sure, and she'll have to show her true face!

In health class—which is where we learn how to be better mortals—Mrs. Williams taught us about something called growth mindset. That's when you don't limit yourself by thinking of yourself as just one thing forever, and take opportunities to learn, develop, and change.

I realized I already have a growth mindset, so I stopped listening. I mean, what's more growth mindset than someone who can turn themselves into anything they like?

Thor really *did* need to listen, however. He's Mr. Fixed Mindset—he's already decided that everything is Loki's fault and nothing can change his mind. He

kept glaring at me all through the school day. He's *still* convinced I stole his hammer.

One thing I don't understand is why he doesn't just pin me down on the floor and fart on my head until I give it back. Since he is so sure I took it!

In the evening, I decided to ask him. Not that I wanted to encourage him in his farting, but it was bothering me. I don't like not knowing things!

Perhaps you're more like Odin than you think . . . ? **!**

After dinner I found Thor lounging on the sofa watching sportsball. He refused to pay me *any* attention until the game finished. Unless you count pushing me to the floor without looking at me as "attention."

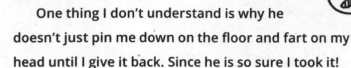

But finally, the game finished and he turned to me with eyes of fire and fury. "What is it, Loki?"

"Why are you in such a foul mood?"

"Because you stole my hammer."

"OK . . . now, don't take this as an invitation to

violence, but . . . if you're so sure of that, why don't you force me to give it back?"

Thor thought about this for a moment. The slow wheels of his mind turned. Eventually, he said:

Perhaps part of me doesn't want to believe you did it. Because I thought you were my friend.
HA! See! You know I didn't do it!

"It's only a *really* small part of me that thinks that," grunted Thor. "Most of me thinks you did it. Because it's *always* your fault."

"Well, most of you will soon be groveling in apology," I said. Honestly, it's disgraceful that Thor assumes everything is my fault, just because I happen to have pulled a *few* tricks on the other gods over the years.

> **!** **Correction: More than a few. Centipedes don't have enough feet to count your many misdeeds and outrages against the gods.**

Centipedes can't count, so I don't need to engage with that nonsense. Just because this diary channels the wisdom and knowledge of Odin himself doesn't mean I have to sit here and be insulted by it!

Correction: It really does. !

Well, I'm closing in on solving this crime, and I will be proved innocent and victorious! Nothing can possibly go wrong!

Correction: The Norns, those celestial beings who govern all our fates, would beg to differ . . . !

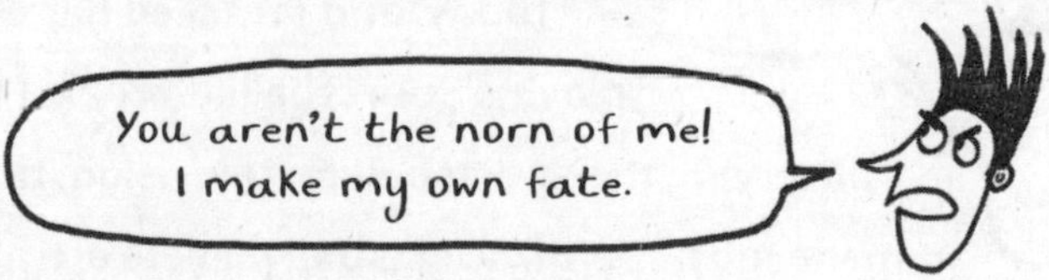

You aren't the norn of me! I make my own fate.

That's what I'm worried about . . . !

Day Twelve

Friday

LOKI VIRTUE SCORE OR LVS:

-300

Plus 50 points for being almost nice to Thor and using your words and not tricks

Georgina was back at school today, and I tracked her down playing sportsball at break. From observing the sportsball on television, this made me hopeful. Sportsball players are always spitting on the floor. So I hovered around the edges of the playground waiting for her to provide the sample I needed.

But she did not spit even once! She's clearly never going to have a career as a professional sportsball player! Shame on her!

Sorry, Kid. No spit, no contract.
Sportsball manager

However, I had a plan.

Do you have a riding lesson tomorrow?

Yes

Will Georgina be there? I would LOVE to get to know her better!

She will, and I'd love that.

👍

And by 👍 I meant: "Mwahahahaha! That giant is in my clutches now!"

Aren't I just the slipperiest trickster there ever was?

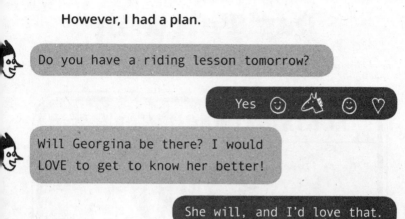

Day Thirteen

Saturday

LOKI VIRTUE SCORE OR LVS:

–300

Holding steady but I sense a fall coming . . .

At the stables, I found Valerie waiting for me.

Well, I *was* overjoyed . . . to prove she was an evil friend-stealing giant.

I waited an eternity for them to return.

You have all the patience of a small human toddler. **!**

I'm ignoring that. While I waited, I told the nearest horse she was a good horse, and she seemed to appreciate it. Finally, I spotted Georgina, walking arm in arm with Valerie toward me. I shuddered, knowing what she truly was.

I needed to find the right moment to encourage Georgina to spit into the small plastic tub I'd brought for this purpose. I had not, it has to be said, come up with an actual plan ahead of time. But I am Loki the great trickster. I have no need of forward planning.

And, lo, a plan came to me in that moment. Georgina was clutching a water bottle and taking swigs as she and Valerie talked.

"Could I have a drink?" I asked.

She looked a little concerned.

I shook my head. While it was theoretically possible for me to get sick in this puny mortal body, it hadn't happened yet!

She looked skeptical, but eventually handed the bottle over.

I grinned. "I have many skills," I said. "Excuse me, I believe I need to go to the restroom now."

"Not surprised," said Georgina, laughing. "They're over there."

I went in the direction she pointed, clutching the water bottle containing Georgina the giant's spit. In my divine hands I held the evidence I needed to prove once and for all that Georgina was the villain of the story!

The crime was so close to being solved! I would be proved innocent! And, more importantly, the friend stealer would be proved *guilty*.

Everything's coming up Loki!

I found a secluded spot behind the stables and placed the open water bottle on the floor. Spell ingredient number one.

Now for ingredients two and three . . .

TRANS-
FORM
Must think of something sad.
One day chips won't exist.
SOB
SOB
TRANS-
FORM
BARK
BARK

The spell was complete! In my human form, I put the lid back on and shook the bottle a little to mix the ingredients, then waited.

ooo

And waited.

ooo

And waited.

ooo

The water did *not* turn blue.

ooo

Which could only mean . . .

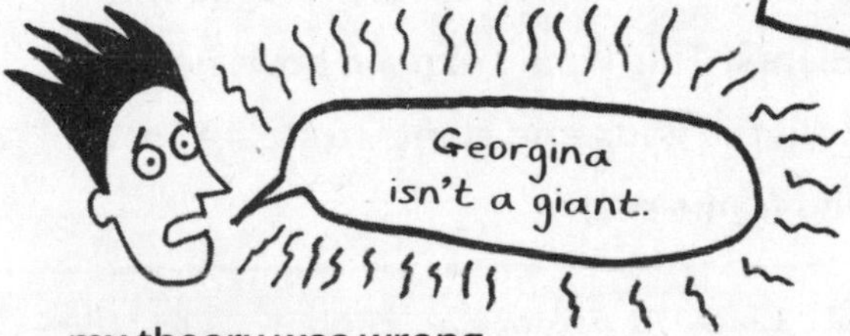

Georgina isn't a giant.

my theory was wrong.

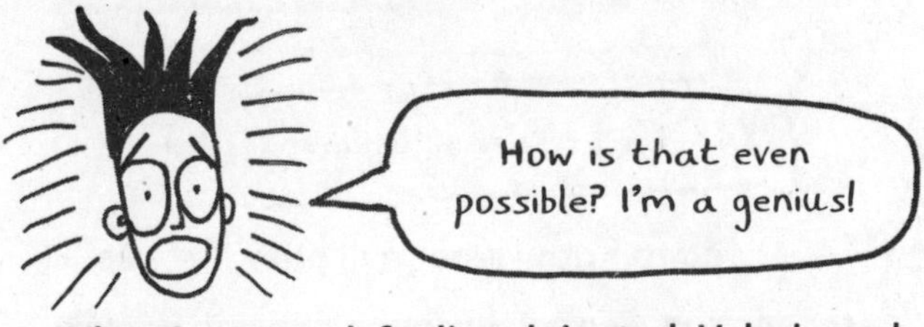

How is that even possible? I'm a genius!

When I returned, feeling dejected, Valerie and Georgina were busy performing child labor. The stench was unbearable, and yet they appeared to be having the time of their lives. They were giggling and telling jokes and whispering.

"Oh, you want to know something really weird?" Valerie was saying to Georgina. "I found a tree covered in frost in the stable yard just now. Even though it's only autumn and it's so warm out today!"

"Climate change?" suggested Georgina.

But I had another theory. Georgina might not be a giant, but maybe she was working *for* the giants. Maybe she was a mortal sorceress in league with the Frost Giants? This would explain how she knew enough about the gods and giants to steal Thor's hammer and frame me!

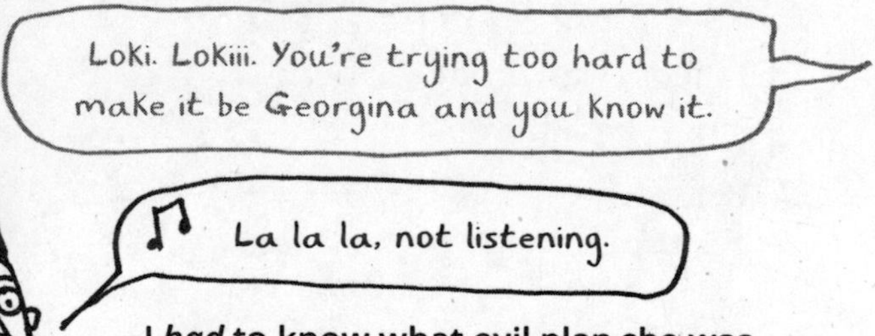

Loki. Lokiii. You're trying too hard to make it be Georgina and you know it.
La la la, not listening.

I *had* to know what evil plan she was concocting. Especially when she and Valerie started one of their play fights, throwing straw at each other and ignoring me.

I waited until Valerie went to the restroom and cornered the villain of the piece.

A tickle of doubt began to form in my mind.

Began to form? I've been here the *whole time*.

"Who's Thor?" asked Georgina.

She was *very* good at playing innocent, wasn't she?

She leaned toward me, irritated. "I don't know what you're accusing me of. What's your problem?" She looked at me like I'd grown another head and the head was upsettingly small and covered in teeth.

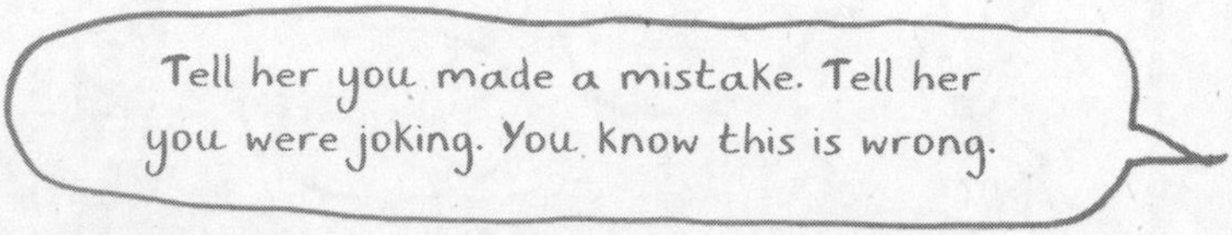

Tell her you made a mistake. Tell her you were joking. You know this is wrong.

To spite that stupid voice, I made my accusation louder and more specific.

I know you took the enchanted hammer of Thor the thunder god!

Are you OK? Should I call your parents?

Tragically, as the lord of lies, master of deception, and sneakiest of gods, I can recognize sincerity when I see it.

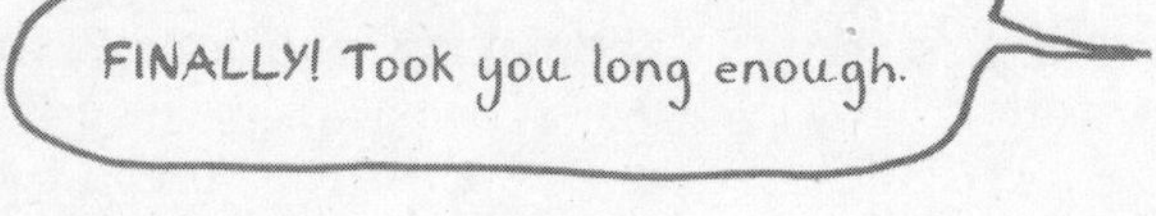

FINALLY! Took you long enough.

I had to admit to myself, against every instinct that told me this friend stealer was guilty, that she . . . wasn't. She was guilty of friend-stealing of course, but not of hammer theft. I could read it in her face. Along with confusion, annoyance, and a hint of fear.

That's when Valerie came back.

"Yeah. But I don't think Liam is. He accused me of stealing some magical hammer? And something about gods?"

Valerie grabbed my arm and pulled me into a corner, whispering so Georgina couldn't hear. "You're not supposed to tell people about the gods! Won't Odin be angry?"

I realized, with a stab of panic, that she was correct. I had a big problem. I had just spoken openly to a mortal about the existence of gods! That was something Odin forbade me from doing, on pain of eternal snake torture. In my defense, I had assumed Georgina

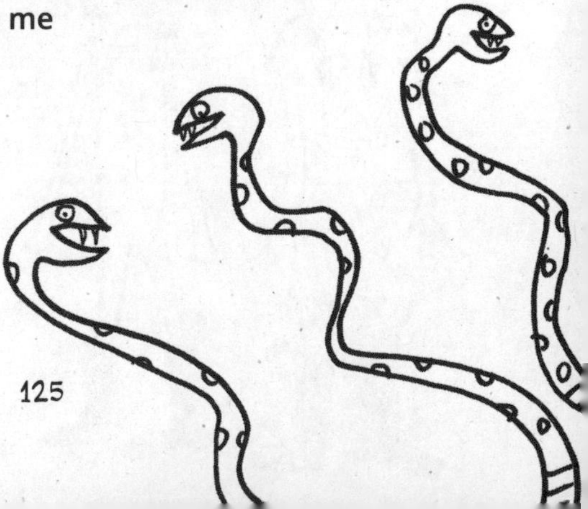

already knew all about the gods because she was in league with the giants, but I suspect that wouldn't be good enough for Odin. He's definitely the smite-first-ask-questions-later type.

Time for some very quick thinking.

"Ahahahahahaha, just kidding," I said, stepping back toward Georgina. "A little inside joke between me and my brother, Thomas. He's so popular I joke that he's a god."

Not my finest cover-up, but it would do in a pinch.

Valerie, thank Odin, went with it. "Yes, you know brothers and their inside jokes," she said.

"Oh. Right. So . . . what part of the joke involves me stealing his hammer?" asked Georgina. She was starting to look angry as well as confused.

"Never mind, it's a long story. I'd have to explain the whole inside joke," I said. "And the moment you explain jokes, they stop being funny."

Georgina's eyes glistened.

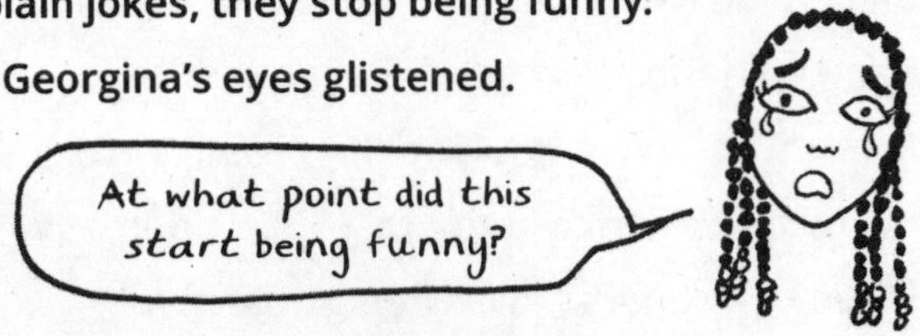

At what point did this start being funny?

Well, I suppose that was a win. She clearly did not suspect that I truly *was* a god, since she changed the subject and suggested we go and see Rusty, the pony Valerie rides.

"You go ahead," Valerie said. "I'll be there in a minute. I just need to tell Liam something."

Georgina nodded and left.

I smiled. "Ah, thank goodness. I thought she'd never leave. Now that we know she didn't do it, let's discuss the next steps in the case of the missing hammer—"

"*Stop!*" hissed Valerie. "Shut up."

I was shocked enough to do so. She had fury in her eyes.

"I can't believe you went behind my back and accused Georgina," she said. "Why?"

"Because she was clearly guilty!" I said.

"She clearly isn't! And I don't think guilt's got anything to do with it. I think you're jealous that I have a new friend."

"No, no, no, that's not it at all!" I said. "I was just following the evidence in the case, like a detective! And it led to Georgina! I was being objective!"

"No, you weren't," said Valerie. "You're being . . . you're being . . . LOKI!" she spat. "I'm starting to think you really haven't changed at all."

"I have! I'm a Good God™ now!" I said.

"So you say. But it's not how you act," said Valerie.

And she strode away, leaving me all alone. Well, except for the ponies, but they weren't much help.

Day Fourteen

Sunday

LOKI VIRTUE SCORE OR LVS:

-1300

Thought so. 1000 points lost for falsely accusing Georgina AND ignoring your conscience.

I'm too wretched to argue with you.

No texts from Valerie. A day of barren despair. Well, barren despair and watching videos of a baby falling over onto a cake. Then I watched a video of a cat being surprised by a snake. But even that couldn't lift my spirits.

If you are tired of surprised cats, Loki, you are tired of life.

And, to add insult to injury, I tried cruelly taunting strangers on the internet and it . . . brought me no joy.

Apparently becoming a Good God™ also means losing thrills that previously set my heart on fire with song.

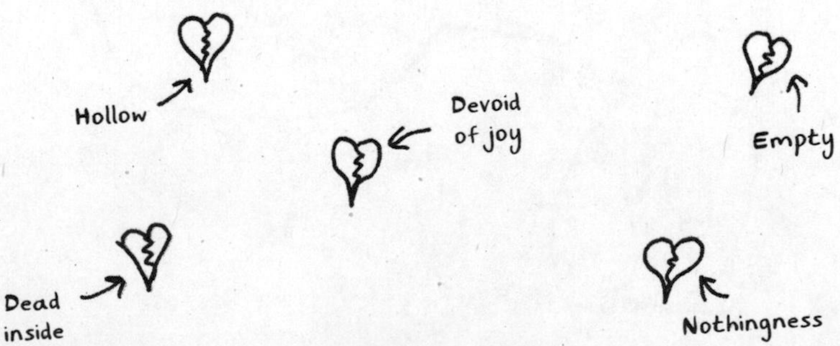

Day Fifteen

Monday

LOKI VIRTUE SCORE OR LVS:

-1350

50 points lost for torturing strangers on the internet. Yes, even though you didn't enjoy it, it still counts.

I checked my phone first thing.

It was full of sorrow and silence.

Hyrrokkin was giving me pitying looks at breakfast. "You look sad, little Loki," she said, brushing my hair back from my face. Humph. I had specifically brushed it forward to hide my tears!

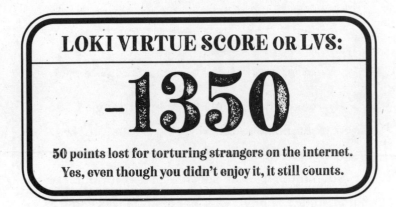

"I'm *fine*," I mumbled.

"If you say so," said Hyrrokkin.

I nodded and swallowed a mouthful of mushy cereal.

You can't be fine if you're eating me.

Hyrrokkin then cut my toast into triangles. I don't know what mortal witchcraft this is, but it makes toast taste better.

But although it was delicious, I was furious. I was *not* an object of pity. I was a *god*! And I was going to prove I was innocent and someone else was guilty and everyone was going to love me again. Especially Valerie. All would be forgiven and forgotten as soon as I solved this stupid crime.

! **Loki, this diary will not let you lie. But I fear you are far from being honest with yourself.**

PFFFT.

! **You can't *pffft* away reality.**

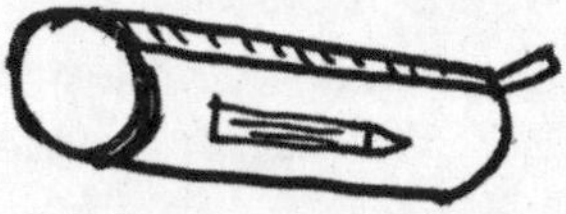

Just watch me.

In spelling, Valerie sat on the opposite side of the room from me, even though I'd saved her a seat using my pencil case. My insides felt like the cold and barren landscape of Hel itself. Then, on his way to take his seat with his fellow sportsboys, Thor gave me a pitying look. "So, your only friend has finally abandoned you? I suppose it was inevitable."

This insult only renewed my desire to solve this stupid crime and prove I am better than everyone else. Surely that was the only way to ensure Valerie would like me again?

I looked over at Sarah. She was my only remaining suspect, so it *had* to be her. But why would she steal Thor's hammer?

Search WHY WOULD SOMEONE STEAL A HAMMER IF SHE DOESN'T KNOW IT'S MAGICAL?

Search DOES SHE KNOW IT'S MAGICAL BECAUSE SHE'S WORKING WITH THE GIANTS?

Search TELL ME! I NEED TO KNOW! THERE MUST BE A REASON!

Search PLEASE HELP ME—I'M DOING THIS ALL ON MY OWN AND I HAVE NO FRIENDS.

Rats. There were no answers that were helpful to me. Only ads.

Speaking of ads, Thor started laying into me on the way home as we passed that stupid Hammerswap ad again.

Honestly, Thor could at least *try* to have some faith in me.

Perhaps you should try harder to give him a REASON to have some faith in you? !

Maybe your face should try harder.

No word from Valerie still. Not a single text. I bet she's spending the evening texting funny pictures of animals to Georgina. She used to text *me* funny pictures. I have no one to text funny pictures to.

Search CAN YOU SEND YOURSELF A TEXT?

Day Sixteen

Tuesday

LOKI VIRTUE SCORE OR LVS:

-1350

Holding steady

I tried to talk to Valerie in math and at break, but she pretended not to hear me. So I threw myself into my work.

Not my schoolwork, obviously. My detective work.

I spent my breaks in the form of a beetle, following Sarah around, in case she gave away any clues.

What are you hiding, you criminal mastermind?

But she only did boring mortal child things; nothing that screamed, "I am a villain and a genius who commits crimes against the immortal gods!"

At the end of the day, I noticed that her bag was still hanging on its peg as I passed. Everyone else had left and there was no sign of Sarah, so I searched it.

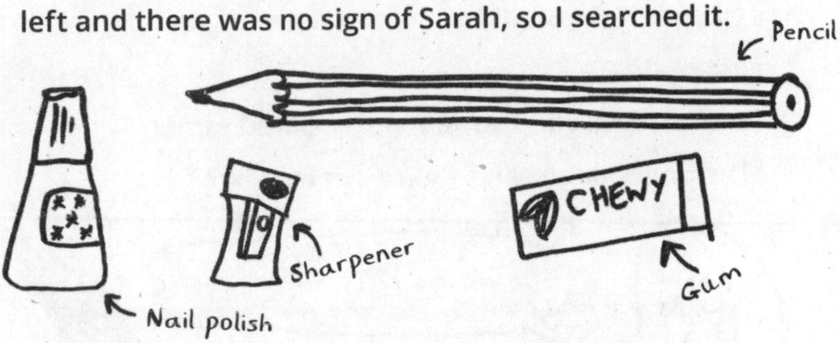

Wait. There was something else in the bag. I felt around and pulled out . . .

Not just any comb. My comb. With a strand of my black hair still wrapped around the teeth!

"What are you doing with my bag?" said a voice behind me.

I turned around and saw Sarah standing there. Busted. So I went on the offensive. "I know you stole my brother's hammer!"

"Did I?" Sarah didn't seem surprised. *Clearly guilty.*

"Yes! And you framed me!" I glared at her. "The only thing I can't figure out is: Why?"

Her shape began to wobble and blur around the edges. Then she grew and grew and her hair became brighter and her eyes glowed like the goddess that she was.

I am ashamed to say that I gasped.

Sif gave me one of her trademark scowls. "Yes, it's me," she said.

"But . . . why did you steal Thor's hammer and frame me?" I demanded.

At that, Sif flinched. "Wait . . . you're wondering why I would take revenge on the god who has wronged me more than any other?"

"What have I ever done to you?!" I asked.

LIST OF THINGS LOKI HAS DONE TO ME

- Shaved my head
- Stole my jewelry
- Cut down my favorite tree and turned it into an insulting wooden carving of Thor
- Shaved my head AGAIN
- Turned my pet goat into a poisonous toad
- Put a stink bomb in my favorite shoes so everyone would think I had smelly feet
- Came into my chambers in the night and stuck all my furniture to the ceiling

Twenty minutes later, she finally finished listing everything I'd ever done to her. To be quite honest, I'd forgotten half of it and was delighted to be reminded.

"In conclusion," she said, "I took on the form of a mortal child to observe your punishment on Midgard."

I was almost impressed. "How did you pull it off? You're not a shifter! You're a nature goddess!"

"A giant owed me a favor after I saved her from Odin's wrath one time. She performed a spell, allowing me to shift back and forth between these two forms. You're not the only one who has madcap adventures, you know," Sif said with a slight twinkle in her eye. "It didn't take me long to realize you were actually *enjoying* your punishment. You like it here!"

"What? No, I don't!" I said.

"You do. You like chips. And the internet. And having a friend."

OK, that was fair.

She glared at me. "Since Odin failed to punish you properly, I decided you should

be subjected to the same level of embarrassment that I suffered at your hands and decided to humiliate and reject you in front of your new peers. But you didn't get the hint that you were being rejected," she said.

I shrugged.

"I just thought you were shy. After all, who would reject *this*." I gestured to my magnificence.

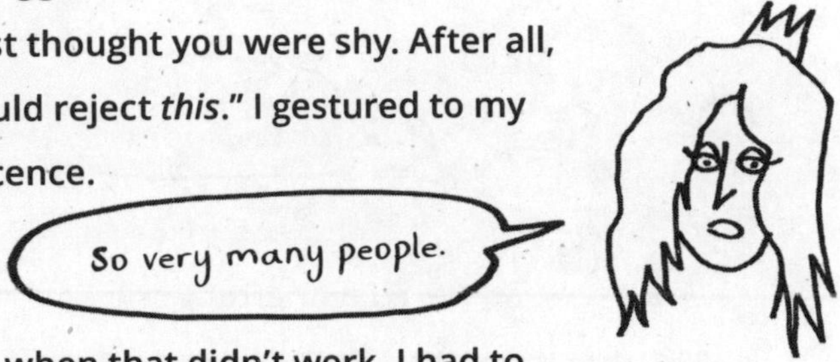

"But when that didn't work, I had to improvise," Sif continued before I could object. "I tried to get you into trouble with your teachers by framing you for a prank. But you enjoyed taking the blame for that."

"That was *you*?" I beamed. "Congratulations, that was excellent and hilarious!"

Sif let out a very weary sigh. "But then I saw you with Heimdall at the gates of school. He was wiping your face with his hanky and I suddenly realized: you have found a family here, one that cares for you, and one you care for in return. Which is more than you deserve, you wretch." She

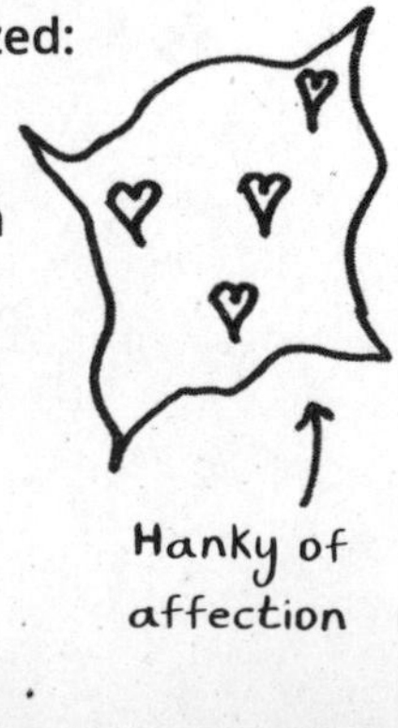

fixed me with her steely gaze. "So . . . I knew the way to punish you: through this family of yours. When you invited me to Thor's party, I planned to steal Thor's hammer and frame you, ensuring your new family hated you. As they *should*."

"Sif, that is fiendish. No, it's dastardly," I said. I bowed low before her. A master of trickery has to recognize another master, even if the other master made the first master's life a living nightmare.

Sif acknowledged my bow with the slightest nod of her head and the smallest twitch of her mouth.

But wait. Something about this wasn't adding up.

"Why are you confessing?" A master of trickery doesn't just own up to their tricks for no reason.

It pains me greatly to say this, but I need your help.
Sorry, you'll have to speak up.
I need your help.
Louder!
I NEED YOUR HELP, OK? ARE YOU HAPPY NOW?

Oh, I was so very happy. This was too sweet. Too beautiful. I wanted to savor every moment.

"Well, well, well," I said, "you need my help, do you? *My* help? Of *course* you do. Loki is the greatest. Loki is the cleverest. Say it."

"Say what?"

"Say 'Loki is the greatest. Loki is the cleverest.' "

Sif gave me a look that could curdle the milk of even the mighty primeval cow Audumla. Thorny weeds started growing up from the ground, and the closest one started to wrap itself around my ankle until I shook it off.

But still, she said it.

LOKI IS THE GREATEST. LOKI IS THE CLEVEREST.

"Now please express that in the form of song and dance," I added.

With a look of fiery fury that could fry every living being from the surface of Midgard, Sif complied. She was *so* angry that the weeds withered and died on the spot!

No dance has ever been more beautiful!

"So why, exactly, do you need the help of the great god Loki?" I asked when she had finished.

Sif looked at her feet. "After I took the hammer, I left it in a safe place. I was planning to wait until your whole family had turned on you, then plant the hammer somewhere, making it look like it was where you'd hidden it. Then, when Thor found it, he'd be convinced you were guilty."

OK, I was impressed. That was *sneaky*.

"And then?" I said.

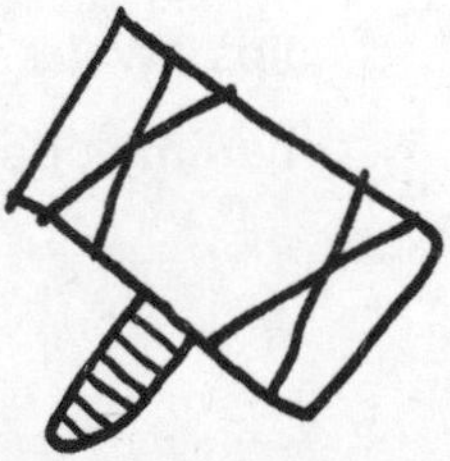

"It turns out that my safe hiding place . . . wasn't such a safe place after all," she said. "Before I had a chance to move it to where Thor could find it, er . . . the Frost Giants did."

Gulp.

"They left a note."

We have the hammer.

IF YOU DON'T GIVE US THOR, WE WILL USE THIS HAMMER TO WREAK HAVOC ON MIDGARD. BRING THOR TO THE INDUSTRIAL PARK AT SUNSET ON THOR'S DAY.*

The Frost Giants

*Aka Thursday to mortals

"I need your help to get it back. Before Odin finds out," she finished.

"And why, exactly, shouldn't I leave you to get punished by Odin? Given that you, oh yes, *framed me for a crime I didn't commit!*"

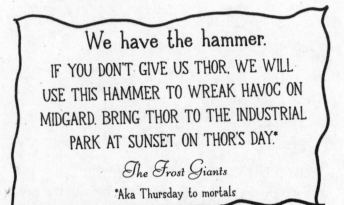

At that, a malicious smile spread over Sif's lips. "Well . . . if Odin finds out the giants have the hammer, don't you think he will blame you for not guarding it better? You are on Midgard to stop this sort of thing from happening, after all."

"Why wouldn't he blame Thor? It's his hammer!" I pointed out.

She gave a sly smile. "Since when does he ever blame Thor, when you're available?"

I thought about this. She did have a point. A very annoying point.

This was fiendish. Sif was more like me than I'd cared to admit! It takes a trickster to trick a trickster, after all.

Before I agreed to help her, we talked terms. She swore a blood oath: that she would confess to Odin and all of Asgard once we had retrieved the hammer. And I swore one in return: that I wouldn't tell on her to Odin until the hammer was safely back in Thor's possession. (Blood oaths are a serious business for us gods. Even I don't break them. Well, maybe once or twice.)

I also made her swear an extra blood oath, that she would perform another song and dance about how I was the best god and the greatest god and all should worship me, even the other gods. She didn't like this oath. I really, really did.

Once we were all agreed and blood-oathed, she changed back into her Sarah form and made to leave.

"Not yet," I said. "I need to show you something at home."

She came with me, highly suspicious. But she needed me, so she was in my power. Oh, how I have missed that feeling. Attempting to be good means missing out on many of the sweeter parts of life. Who needs friendship when you have *this*?

> ! **Do you really mean that, Loki? Don't you miss Valerie?**

Not at all! I hope she's *very* happy with Georgina. Or dead. Who cares?

> ! **Lie detected.**

Look, mine is a high and lonely destiny. I realize that now. Friendship only leads to pain.

When we reached our house, Sif followed me inside, stepping carefully as though I might spring a trap on her at any moment. Which was exactly what I did.

Thor! Sarah's here and she has something to confess!
You swore you wouldn't tell until the hammer was safely returned!
I swore I wouldn't tell *Odin*.

Yes? What is it, Loki?
Sarah...
TRANSFORM
GASP!
So, about your hammer...
I took it.

Thor went through every Thor emotion.

"Sif . . . you took my hammer?" Thor said at last.

"Indeed she did," I said. "Imagine! Your wife betraying you like this!"

(Yes, they're married. Long story . . . actually it's not. They got married. The end.)

"Do you have something you want to say to *me*?" I added.

"Pardon?"

"I'm sorry," he said, louder.

"Sorry for what?" I said. I do love to draw out the humiliation process. The longer it lasts, the sweeter it tastes!

I would like to note that this will be reflected in your virtue score. !

So worth it.

"Sorry for what?" I repeated.

"I'm sorry I assumed you stole my hammer," said Thor.

I bowed, ever so graciously. "Thank you, Thor. Now that wasn't so hard, was it?"

"No," said Thor. Then he turned to look at Sif. "But, my love, why did you take it?"

"To get Loki into trouble as a punishment for cutting off my hair." She folded her arms. "Again."

Thor thought about that. "Well, I suppose that is a good reason. But you shouldn't stoop to his level! So . . . where is my hammer?"

"That's the thing," I said. "Sif let the giants take it."

At that point, Heimdall and Hyrrokkin came running. Heimdall was holding a sword and Hyrrokkin had a spear. Fido brought up the rear, barking his head off.

"Giants? In our house? Why didn't the alarm go off?" boomed Heimdall. He shook his sword angrily. "I'm going to complain to the manufacturer!"

Manufacturer: a group of mortals who make things for other mortals to buy. A manufacturer is like a dwarven smithy, only the things a manufacturer makes usually go wrong. The products are designed this way on purpose, so you are forced to buy new wrong-going things.

"Where are they?" growled Hyrrokkin. She glared around the giant-free room until her eyes rested on . . .

"Wait . . . Sif, what are you doing here?" asked Heimdall.

There was a lot of explaining to do. But explanations are *much* more fun when the humiliating chaotic mess is not your fault.

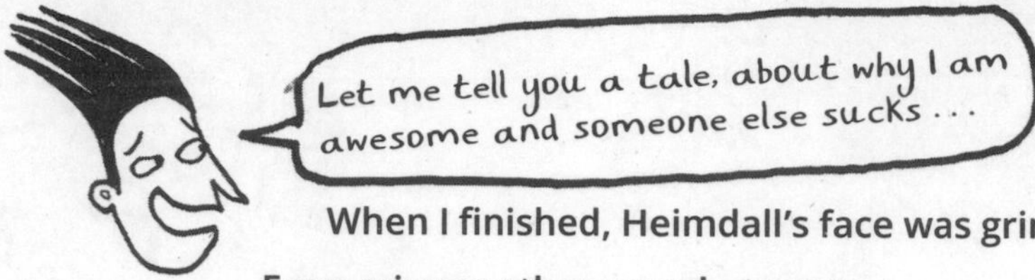
Let me tell you a tale, about why I am awesome and someone else sucks . . .

When I finished, Heimdall's face was grim.

Even grimmer than usual, anyway.

"This is bad," he said. "That hammer magnifies the power of Thor. Who knows what a powerful Frost Giant could do with it?"

Hyrrokkin nodded. "They could do terrible things. To the gods . . ."

Whatever. The gods could do terrible things right back. And often have.

". . . and to mortals . . ." Hyrrokkin added.

Mortals? Pah. I cared nothing for mortals.

Mortals suck.
Except Valerie . . .
Oh no!
Valerie is in danger!

"We need to get Thor's hammer back," I said. Not that I cared about Valerie now that she'd abandoned me.

That's a big fat lie. **!**

"Anyhow, hold your eight-legged horses," said Hyrrokkin. "You need a plan! You don't have your hammer to fight the Frost Giants, remember!"

Thor grumbled, but we all sat down at the kitchen table. Heimdall made us some hot drinks and put out a plate of cookies. I think they were "sorry we assumed you were guilty" flavor. Thor didn't seem to realize that they were clearly for me, the wronged party, and took five.

Then Heimdall made us dinner. It was marginally less disgusting than usual. We discussed possible plans to get the hammer back but nothing seemed right. Especially not Thor's "Should I just charge?" plan, which he brought out again. Before we knew it, it was bedtime!

"Would you like to stay the night, Sif?" Heimdall asked.

Sif shook her head. "No offense, but my earthly dwelling is ever so slightly more luxurious than this."

"Where *are* you staying?" asked Hyrrokkin.

"In a five-star hotel, of course. With a jacuzzi and spa and a movie theater and room service. Where did you *think* a goddess would stay while on Earth?"

OMG, SO UNFAIR!

"Right. Off to bed. We will all plan together in the morning," said Hyrrokkin.

"NO!" said Heimdall, in the same tone of voice he would use while guarding the rainbow bridge against particularly nasty trolls. "Hyrrokkin, they should come up with their own plan. We should not allow them to rely on their elders to fight their battles for them."

"Technically, we're about the same age . . ." I began, but he was clearly not in the mood for a lecture.

"In *Twelve Rules for Parents*, Dr. Patterson says that boys need to learn independence and a sense of personal responsibility. And clean their rooms . . ."

I don't see why I should help. None of this is my fault.

If you had left your hammer somewhere safe, we wouldn't be in this mess.

I snickered. This was fun.

"And no laughing from you, Loki," said Heimdall. "Even though you didn't steal the hammer, it is your Odin-given duty to protect the mortal realm from Frost Giants!"

Sif, wisely, stayed *very* quiet and avoided Heimdall's wrath. But, in summary, we weren't getting any help from Heimdall and Hyrrokkin to beat the giants.

"Very well," I said. "We shall assemble tomorrow to come up with a plan!"

"After school," said Heimdall.

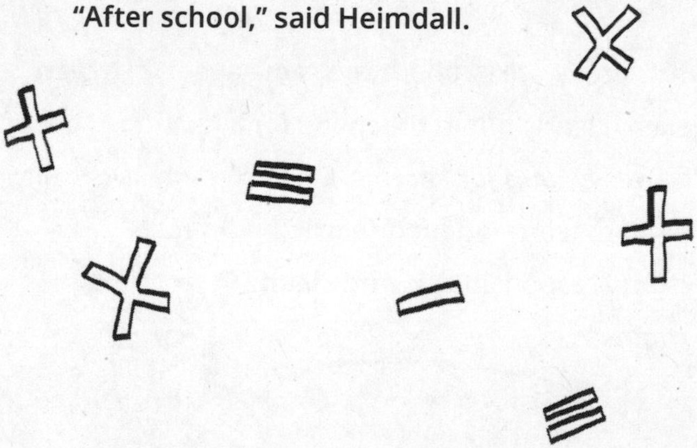

Day Seventeen

Wednesday

LOKI VIRTUE SCORE OR LVS:

-1500

Points deducted for humiliating Sif and stealing nail polish from her bag

What can I say?
I look good in it.

During drama, the teacher paired me with Valerie. Score! A chance to make her talk to me!

We had to read out a scene from a play about a prince dressing up as a poor person and everyone being fooled by a mere costume change. Mortals are very stupid.

I tried to strike up a conversation, making a witty observation about the ridiculousness of the play's plot.

"Let's just read the lines," hissed Valerie.

"But—"

"Alas, I am but a humble peasant," said Valerie, reading from her script.

I sighed. Her ignoring me was getting tedious. I needed a scheme to get her to like me again.

Of course, being a genius, I came up with one almost immediately. Honestly, this idea was so stunningly brilliant that I genuinely don't know how my mortal brain could handle it without collapsing in a pile of goo.

I couldn't talk to her . . . but someone *else* could. Someone she had no reason to distrust or be irrationally angry with. As I said, I can be literally anything or *anyone* I want. Time to bring out the big guns.

SWELL
GROW
EMBLONDEN
SHRINKKK
Hmm . . .
That's better.
BIG GUNS

Taking on Thor's human form felt much stranger than my usual transformations. As a horse or a fly or a girl, I'd never been on the receiving end of The Look. It was like being bathed in glory streaming from the eye-beams of all who beheld me. No wonder Thor was so sure of himself. It's cheating, frankly.

On the plus side, it made it easier to adopt his swaggering walk. The Look even inspired me to try some tricks with a soccer ball as I passed through the playground. Sadly, while my transformation guaranteed me Thor's strength and speed, it did not lend me his skill.

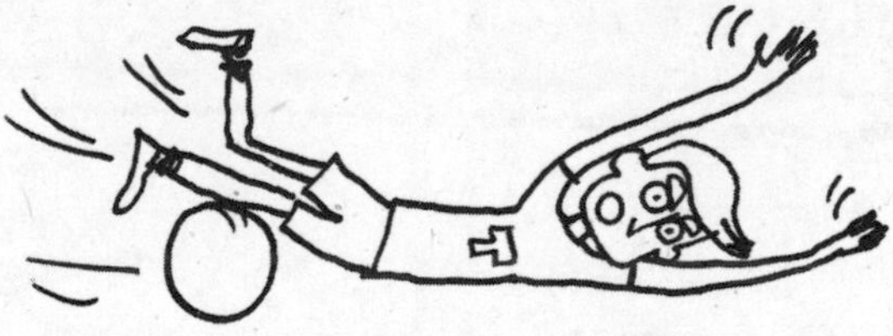

After that brief humiliation—which was damaging to Thor's reputation, not mine—I found Valerie. She was in the school library reading a book about alien abductions.

I put on a very low and serious Thor voice. "Valerie, can we talk?"

Valerie looked up. "Is Loki OK?"

I felt a glow in my borrowed heart.

"He's fine. More than fine," I said. "Handsome as ever."

Valerie sighed deeply.

"Oh no, did the black hair come back?" I patted my head in irritation.

"No. But Thor would never call you handsome. No one says the word *handsome* as much as you do. About yourself mostly."

She closed her book. "What do you want?"

"I came to warn you that you're in danger," I said, with all the drama I could muster. Which was a lot. "So you have to be my best friend again for your own protection."

This did not get the response I expected. I expected a mix of shock and gratitude.

What I got was pure disgust.

100% PURE
DISGUST — NOT
MADE FROM
CONCENTRATE

She sighed deeply. "This is a trick, isn't it? You just want me to forget that you accused my friend of theft and not have to deal with the fact that you did something bad by creating fake danger."

"No! I mean, yes, I want all that," I said. "But it's real danger! The person who stole the hammer was the goddess Sif in disguise and now the Frost Giants have Thor's hammer and they're going to use it to . . . well, I'm not exactly sure. But it's going to be bad."

Valerie shook her head. "Even if you're *not* making all that up—and it sounds made up—I don't think you're actually worried about me. You just want an excuse for everything to be OK between us. It's not. Go away, Loki. Come back when you're ready to apologize."

Then she glared at me until I had to slink away to turn back into my own form in the restroom.

When school ended, eons later, Sif walked home with me and Thor. When we got to the house, Thor barreled into the hallway without taking off his muddy shoes, like the brute he is.

Once inside, we settled down on the scruffy sofa.

Heimdall bustled off to get us refreshments while Thor opened with an idiotic suggestion.

"When we get to the meeting place, I could attack the giants with my mighty bare fists and grab Mjolnir."

"I doubt they'd be foolish enough to bring the hammer to the industrial park," pointed out Sif.

"*I* would bring the hammer if I were them," said Thor. "Saves two trips."

"You've rather proved Sif's point there," I said.

Only I get to insult my husband.

We squabbled for a bit, but then I suggested looking at the giants' note for clues.

Sif took it from her schoolbag and put it down on the coffee table for us all to look at.

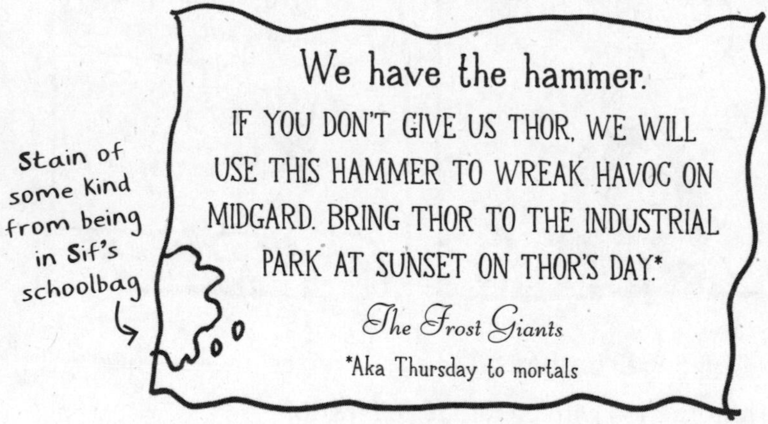
We have the hammer.
IF YOU DON'T GIVE US THOR, WE WILL USE THIS HAMMER TO WREAK HAVOC ON MIDGARD. BRING THOR TO THE INDUSTRIAL PARK AT SUNSET ON THOR'S DAY.*
The Frost Giants
*Aka Thursday to mortals
Stain of some kind from being in Sif's schoolbag

The note gave nothing away, other than the fact that Sif is not very good at keeping notes clean.

We had until tomorrow to come up with a plan from scratch. We all sat in thoughtful silence. Well, Sif and I were in thoughtful silence. I imagine the inside of Thor's mind looked something like this: →

Actually, that was it! "I have a genius plan," I said.

Thor and Sif looked at me with something less than adoration and worship in their eyes. But they'd be *flooded* with admiration when I told them my plan.

Unfortunately, I was interrupted by Heimdall coming in with cookies.

(On the plus side: cookies.)

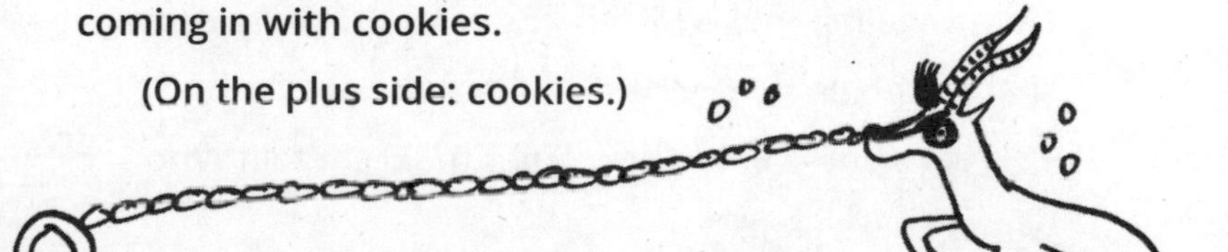

"So, here's how it will go . . ." I said, and explained my genius plan. It involved trickery (me), treachery (against the giants), and transformation (me and Thor). "In conclusion, Thor will escape his chains after I have transformed him into a fly, and we shall steal the hammer from their lair."

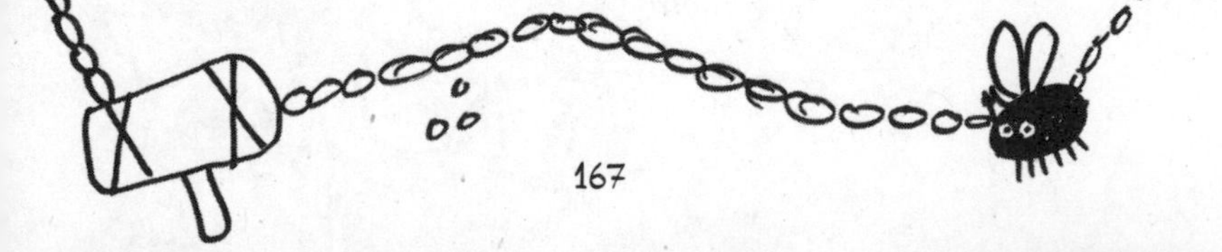

Sif frowned. "That sounds really complicated. The more parts in a plan, the more likely it is to go wrong."

"I agree," said Thor. "I don't like complicated plans. I like hitting things with hammers."

"Let's go to the meeting place and hide, then follow them home to their lair," said Sif.

"Great idea, my wife!" said Thor.

Sif smiled, and the green bananas in a bowl on the table ripened to a rich yellow. So smug.

The annoying married ones were siding against me! Which made me even *more* certain that my plan was the best.

"Let's vote," said Thor. "That makes it fair. Who wants Loki's plan?"

I put my hand up. No one else did.

"And Sif's plan?" asked Thor.

They both put their hands up. Heimdall popped back around the door with some more cookies and put his hand up, too.

Custard cream?
Squashed fly cookie?

"I don't eat traitor cookies," I hissed. "Well, maybe just the one . . ."

"Looks like we're going with Sif's plan," said Thor.

Even worse, Sif wasn't going to join us for the plan.

"I'm the brains of the operation," she said. "You can be the brawn for once.

"Besides," Sif added, "When I do mighty deeds, it always gets left out of the stories that mortals tell. There's not one word in the tales about the time I brought down a giant stronghold by choking it with weeds! Nor the time I tamed the great hound Garm, guardian of Hel, with the scent of sweet flowers! So I might as well take it easy for once."

This was true. In the written mortal records of our amazing adventures, Sif's role can be more or less summed up as "gets her hair cut off by Loki and is married to Thor." I suspect this is because of a mortal concept called sexism.

Sexism: the foolish mortal idea that the world is divided into men and women and that men are superior. Mortals even pretend things are male and female that don't have living bodies: for example, ships.

What nonsense! After all, I'm both male and female at different times, and I'm equally awesome in both forms! And ships are inanimate objects! Mortals are often very, very silly. I have a mind to rewrite all the stories about us Norse gods and tell the ones that have been left out, including Sif's many adventures. Especially the ones that involve ME.

Anyway. Our plan was in place. And after we were victorious, I could focus on the truly important task of getting Valerie to be my best friend again and hearing her admit I am a Good God™ who can do no wrong.

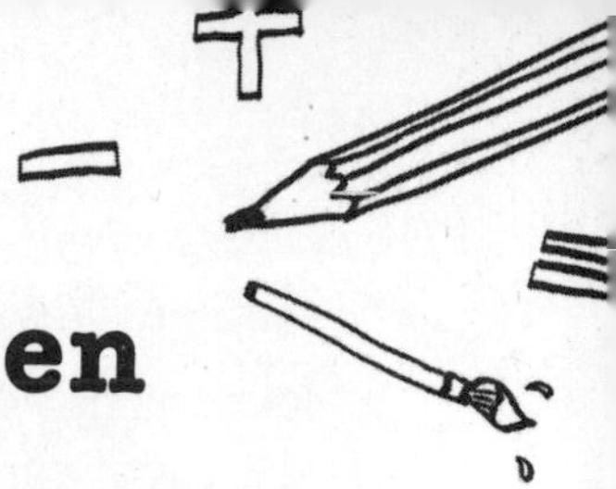

Day Eighteen

Thursday

LOKI VIRTUE SCORE OR LVS:

-1500

Holding steady but could nosedive at any moment . . .

One thing I have discovered about mortal life is that when you have something important to do at the end of a school day, every single lesson seems to last one million years.

Amount of time between the continents forming and now.

Amount of time between start and end of the school day.

Finally, after several ice ages had passed, Thor and I headed home.

There was an hour to kill before sunset, and Heimdall decided it was a good moment for some “family time” before we ate.

Like the school day, family time always seems to last longer than it should. It involves “character-building” activities such as crafts, and no actually enjoyable activities, such as watching TV or playing video games. I made a papier-mâché sculpture of a poop, in protest.

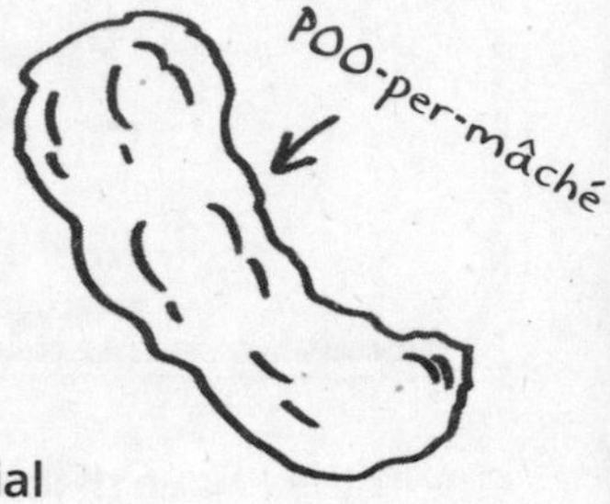

Finally, the ordeal was over and we were allowed to eat. I walked with Thor to the industrial park, where we climbed some metal stairs and hid on the roof of a building.

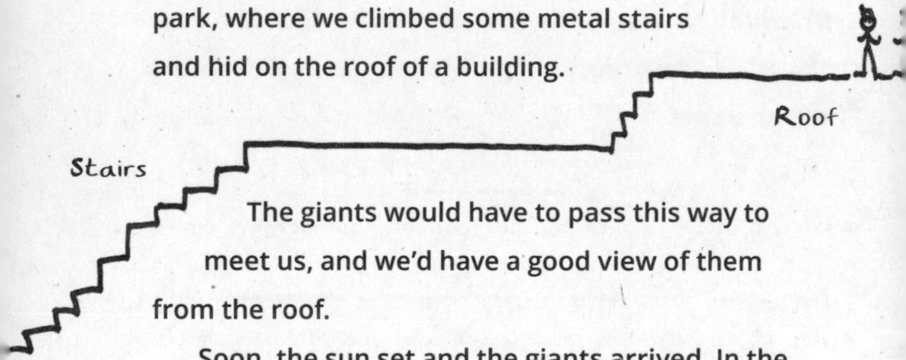

The giants would have to pass this way to meet us, and we’d have a good view of them from the roof.

Soon, the sun set and the giants arrived. In the dim light I recognized them as the Frost Giants who we defeated last month!

"Great, now all we need to do is wait for them to get bored and go away. Then we can follow them," said Thor. He shook his head and a sappy smile spread over his face. "Sif is so clever. This is such a good plan! I feel very honored to have her for my wife. Perhaps you should get married, Loki. It's a shame your godly form is so off-putting that no one would have you . . ."

And that was the point I made my decision.

"OK, just follow my lead," I hissed at Thor. "We're switching to my plan! Sif's is terrible!"

"What?" said Thor. "No, Loki, we agreed—"

"Hush, you should be more flexible," I said. "Growth mindset and whatnot."

"But—"

I stood up and went to the edge of the roof.

HEY! UP HERE! I'VE GOT THOR! COME AND GET HIM!

The giants looked in our direction and roared. Then they started running up the metal stairs.

"Loki! You don't understand, this is *not* a tactically defensible position!"

The only time Thor uses long words is when he's talking about military strategy. I don't like military strategy. I prefer thinking on my feet.

And as the giants reached the top of the stairs, I suddenly realized that we were trapped on the roof with the giants with no way out.

I told you so!

Aha, but one god's trap is another god's master plan! I did not *want* to escape. I wanted them to lead us to the hammer!

“So, I have betrayed Thor once again, as is my way,” I said breezily. But before I could go on to subtly inquire about the location of the evil lair where they had the hammer stashed, General Glacier shook her sharp-clawed finger.

“Oh, Loki, Loki, we’re not going to fall for that.”

“Fall for what? I’m betraying Thor. Betraying the gods is my thing. My personal brand. One hundred percent what I’d do. I’ve done it before and I’ll do it again.”

How gullible do you think I am?

This wasn’t going the way I’d hoped.

“Loki, I think we need to start fighting,” hissed Thor.

“No, I just need time to think!”

Come on, brain, don’t fail me now! You are a GENIUS, remember!
BLEEP BLOOP BRRRR BLIP BLIP DOOBY DOOO ERROR PLEASE REBOOT

I had a sudden horrible feeling that maybe Sif had been right all along about my plan.

Horrible because other people being right is horrible. And also horrible because the giants had us surrounded.

But all was not lost! I could still do the escaping part of the plan! I changed into a bird, then . . .

SNAP

Chains closed around Thor's wrists. I tried to change him into a tiny creature so he could fall out of the chains, but something was stopping me.

AAARGH! Magic! Stupid magical chains!

"LOKI!" roared Thor. "This is your fault!"

I swooped above him, plotting my next move.

I decided that a rescue would have to wait, but I could at least follow the giants to their lair. Which was part of my plan anyway. So, really, I was winning!

> **! Thor trapped in magical chains? Your definition of "winning" is unusual, to say the least.**

Ahem, as I was saying before I was so rudely yet accurately interrupted . . .

I followed the giants from a safe distance as they trudged into some scraggly woodland. The place would have been beautiful had it not been full of refuse left behind by humans, who invented garbage bins and yet seem incapable of using them. The giants stopped when they reached an abandoned cottage and shoved Thor inside, locking the door. The giants then proceeded to argue about who would guard Thor and who would go back to the lair.

Captain Icebeard drew the short straw (not literally, the Frost Giants decided who would stay by having a fistfight) and stood guard outside Thor's cottage.

I decided to follow the others to the lair.

Then I could fly home in triumph claiming that this had all been part of my plan so I could discover the giants' lair where they must be keeping the hammer. Yes, I would be victorious! I swooped down, doing a little loop the loop of self-congratulation . . .

When I came to, there was no sign of the giants, except for Captain Icebeard looking grumpy as he stood guard outside the cottage.

TURDS.

I flew home and through the window of my bedroom so Hyrrokkin and Heimdall couldn't ask me how things had gone.

I decided to go to bed. After all, don't mortals say that "everything looks better in the morning"?

You do realize that going to sleep is not a way to fundamentally alter reality . . . ?

What if I enter a state of mystical divine sleep in which I dream a new universe? Bet you hadn't thought of that!

I had not. But get back to me in the morning if that happens, eh?

Day Nineteen

Friday

LOKI VIRTUE SCORE OR LVS:

-1600

Points lost for putting Thor in harm's way

! Wait . . . Loki? Where are you?

! Loki . . . ?

! What are you playing at?

Day Twenty

Saturday

LOKI VIRTUE SCORE OR LVS:

TBD

Because there is no diary entry from yesterday

If you refuse to write in this diary, I will have to start deducting *many* points— Wait . . . you're writing.

I'm back, I'm back! Don't take away points, please!

Will suspend point judgment until you explain yourself. What happened yesterday? Where are you back from?

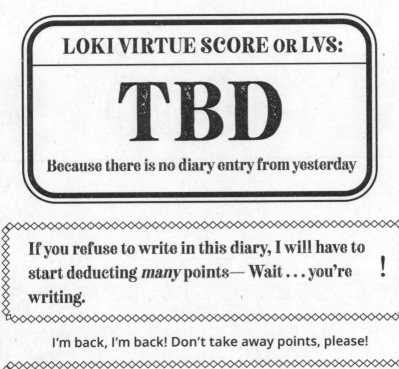

Let's pick up from when I awoke on Friday . . .

Day Nineteen

Friday #2

LOKI VIRTUE SCORE OR LVS:

−1600

Points lost for putting Thor in harm's way

There had been a complete absence of mystical, reality-altering dreams. (Turds!) Though I did dream about being in a snaky dungeon with venom sizzling down upon me, so it was probably a good thing my dreams weren't inclined to come true.

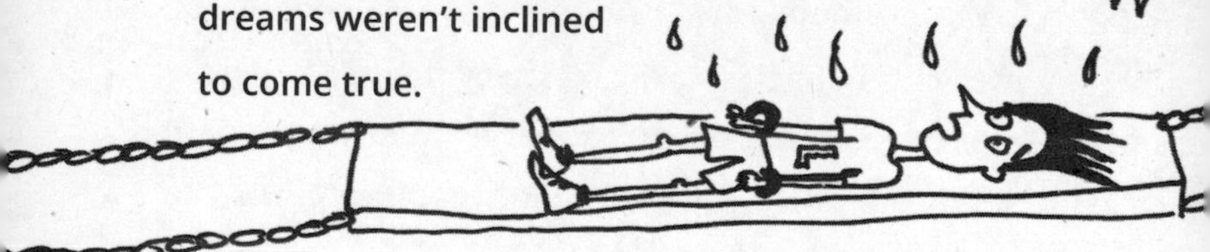

"Time for school!" called Hyrrokkin.

I was still in bed. I planned to stay in bed. There, I didn't have to face the fact that things did *not* look better in the morning. I'd lost Thor to the giants.

The giants still had the hammer. And I wasn't looking forward to explaining this state of affairs to my fake parents. And especially not to Sif.

I turned my phone on, in case Thor had magically texted me saying:

I escaped and this was clearly all part of your master plan, you genius and hero!

He had not. I did, however, have approximately one million texts from Sif asking where we were and what had happened and why Thor wasn't answering his texts. I put my phone down and lay back on the bed in deep despair.

Then I sat bolt upright. I had a brilliant idea that I knew would make everything better and perfect and good. If I rescued Thor *and* got the hammer back at the same time, all would be forgiven and forgotten.

! That sounds highly unlikely. Thor is not the forgiving type.

Hush, no guessing the ending! This is my story!

Here's how I planned to pull off Project Make Everything OK and Force Thor to Forgive Me:

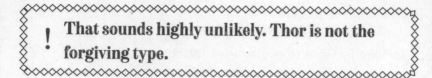

Step 1: Go to cottage where Thor is held.

Step 2: Attack Frost Giant on Thor-guarding duty using trickery to render them terrified and vulnerable.

Step 3: Steal their key and free Thor.

Step 4: Get Thor to intimidate them into telling us where the hammer is.

Step 5: Tell him his capture had all been a bluff.

Step 6: Return victorious and beloved by all!

Simple.

! No, Loki, it's not simple. It's fiendishly complicated and you are not very strong, even in your divine form. This is a bad plan.

As bad as the time I placed a wager that risked getting my head cut off if I didn't win?

OK, not as bad as that. !

Well, then!

I bounded downstairs as soon as I was dressed.

Where's Thor? And would you like some toast?
What happened last night?

"Orange juice or water?" Hyrrokkin added, holding up two jugs from the breakfast table.

But I was ready for their brutal interrogation.

"I can't stop to chat," I said. "Plan went perfectly, but now I need to go. I can't be late for school, can I?"

"But where's Thor?" Heimdall asked.

I pretended not to hear, grabbed two pieces of toast, slugged some orange juice, and ran out the door. I could decide on my full story later. Better not to commit to a cover story until the whole thing is over and you know exactly what you're covering up . . .

I started out in the direction of school but then ducked into an alleyway and transformed into a bird to fly back to the cottage in the woods.

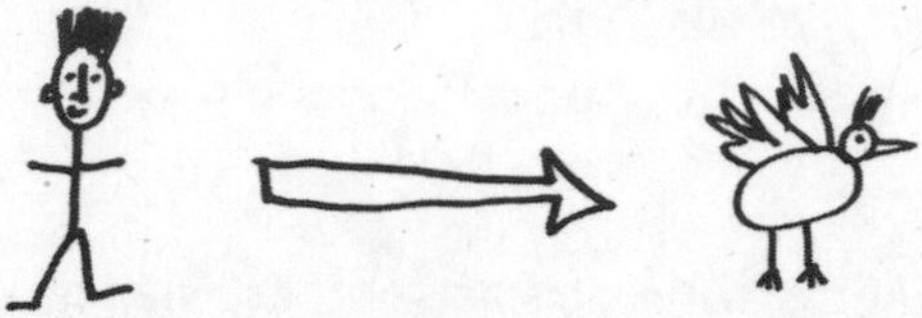

My plan involved complex psychology in order to distract the Frost Giant and steal the keys to the magical cuffs that trapped Thor. I took every Frost Giant's deepest fear . . . and made it come true.

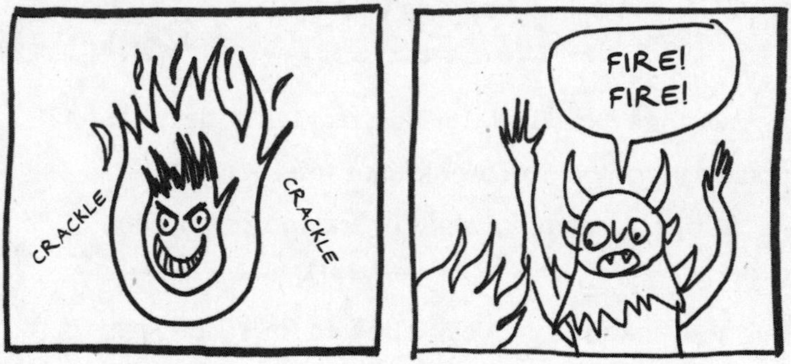

But before I could follow him and demand the location of the hammer while he was in a state of panic and terror . . .

I fell to the ground in boy form—which is when Captain Icebeard grabbed me, clapped me in magical chains, and threw me in the cottage with Thor.

Which I felt wasn't very much in the spirit of developing a growth mindset at *all*.

I admit, this was a low point.

I told you this was a bad plan. **!**

Humph. Do you WANT me to catch you up or what?

! **Proceed.**

So, there we were, trapped.

Don't panic, we have to keep calm!
I AM calm.

The magical chains with which he was bound meant that Thor's lightning was more of a crackle than a **CRACKLE**. I tried turning into every possible creature, object, and substance, but nope. The most I could transform was my hair color, and that faded after five minutes.

Blonds do NOT have more fun.

Thor sighed deeply. "We should summon Odin," he said.

"He's out of Asgard, remember?" I pointed out.

"Oh. Yeah."

Attention to detail is not one of Thor's strengths. Nor is his memory. Except where grudges against me are concerned.

I would have to come up with a plan myself, since Thor was about as much intellectual help as a bag of sausages.

Speaking of sausages, I'd begun to get hungry. I'd only eaten a few bites of my toast before turning into a bird. Thor was clearly hungry, too.

After what felt like years, I heard a noise at the door. (It must have been *loud* because I could hear it over Thor's stomach.) There was some fumbling with the lock, then the door flew open.

"I don't suppose you'd free our hands so we can eat more easily?" I suggested, ever so casually.

"Ha! Do you think I'm stupid, Trickster?"

"Oh no—" I began.

"Come closer and I will kick you!" growled Thor.

"I could *never* consider you stupid in comparison with my present company," I finished.

Captain Icebeard laughed a grunting laugh and handed us our food, none too gently. "You're funny, little god," he said.

"I'm hilarious," I agreed. "Now, since we're such good friends, how about you tell me why you're holding us captive? And, as a bonus, where you've hidden the hammer . . ."

"Ha, ha, ha, nice try," laughed Captain Icebeard.

"Ahhh, I see, I see," I said. "You're not important enough for your boss to tell you the plans. That's OK. You shouldn't feel bad."

"She *does* tell me the plans!" spat Captain Icebeard. "She told me to steal Thor's hammer, but that dratted alarm went off. And she told me to put up posters tempting Thor to bring his hammer to us."

Hammerswap

"None of it worked," Captain Icebeard went on. "But then that goddess stole the hammer and hid it in the basement of your school. Which we know well. It was, like . . . well, a gift from the gods, hur, hur. So, see, Boss *does* tell me the plans!"

He frowned, finally seeing through my ruse. "Oh. I shouldn't have told you that." He loomed over me.

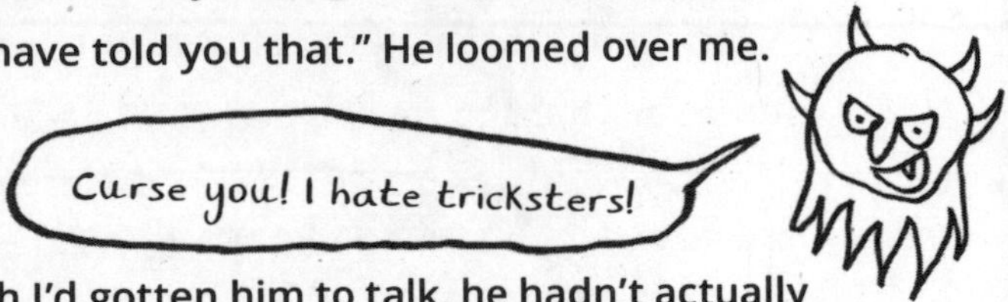
Curse you! I hate tricksters!

Although I'd gotten him to talk, he hadn't actually told me anything useful. This was going to be a challenge. I'd have to use all my cunning.

After lunch, anyway. I was starving.

Thor, bless his predictable heart, tried to kick the giant as he left, but he swerved easily out of the way.

"Ha, ha, ha, ha! Behave, puny child," he said, striding out, slamming the door, and locking it.

"I nearly got him," growled Thor.

"I wish I was writing this in my diary, as my diary would tell you that is a *lie*."

! **I'm not here to correct Thor's lies, only yours.**

BAH.

We sat in grumpy silence and I racked my brains for clever plans and cunning tricks to help us escape. But no plans arrived. Tricks? Zero.

My brain was as blank as Thor's.

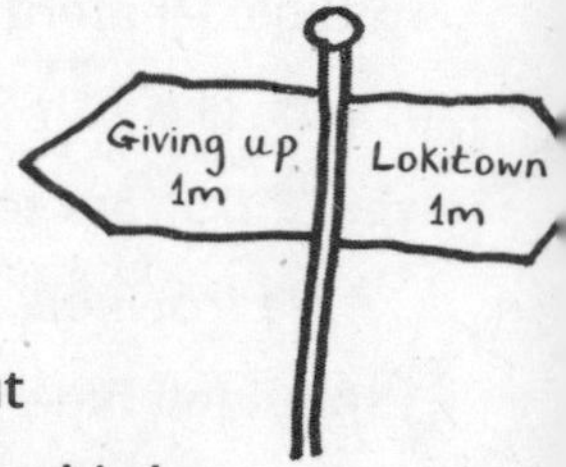

I don't often give up, but I have to confess, I came close to it.

I wished I'd brought my phone. But phones are hard to carry when you're a bird.

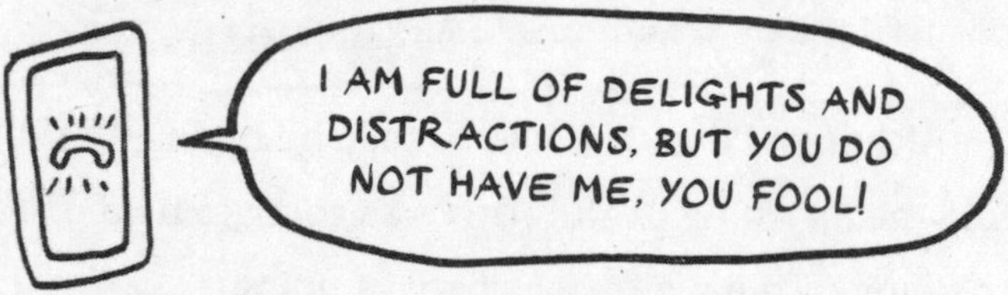

I AM FULL OF DELIGHTS AND DISTRACTIONS, BUT YOU DO NOT HAVE ME, YOU FOOL!

The following hours were deeply tedious and uncomfortable. I don't know if you've ever sat in chains for hours on end, but let me tell you, they chafe. And I was bored.

"Let's play a game," I said to Thor.

No. Let's sit in silence and consider the fact that this is all your fault.

"I don't like that game," I said. "Let's play I Spy."

"I spy with my little eye something beginning with I HATE YOU," growled Thor.

He never was any good at having fun.

Much, much, much, much later, Captain Icebeard brought us another meal, but refused to speak.

TURDS.

I scanned his belt for keys that might unlock our chains, but no such luck.

As I drifted off into uncomfortable sleep, my heart was full of woe. I had no access to magic, my ploys weren't working, Thor was no help . . .

I had to admit it to myself.

I was beaten.

And now we are up to speed for Friday . . .

This diary entry is for SATURDAY.

In which case . . . new entry time! **!**

Day Twenty

Saturday #2

LOKI VIRTUE SCORE OR LVS:

-2600

Minus 1000 points. You know what you did.

I awoke with a start. Someone was at the door.

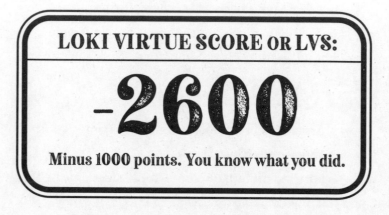

I'm here to rescue you two trollwits.

"Hey!" I said. "I'm not a trollwit! I'm supremely intelligent!"

But I held out my hands, because you don't want to complain too much when someone's rescuing you. Self-Interest 101.

"How did you get the key?" I asked, in a spirit of professional curiosity. Not that I'm a professional thief. Just . . . sometimes I like to acquire things that aren't technically mine through sneaky methods. It's part of the trickster package.

"I didn't," said Sif. "I borrowed Odin's skeleton key that opens everything before I left Asgard."

By then my wrists were free, so I allowed myself a little crowing. "Oh, you are in so much trouble, young lady. Odin is going to roast you. Or possibly freeze you."

But she shushed me. "They could come back at any time. Come on."

She didn't have to ask me twice. I was out of there. Thor followed and Sif brought up the rear, locking the door again. Then we ran.

Thor dashed ahead on his annoyingly mighty legs. Sif kept pace with me, firing questions. She was hardly out of breath, while my lungs felt like they were about to explode. I should send this body back to Odin! Except, unfortunately, I need it at the moment.

As we ran, Sif explained that she'd decided to go looking for us when we didn't turn up for school. She asked the grass and flowers to find her beloved husband. (Nature goddess perks. A little like the mortal notion of Find My Phone. Only Thor isn't as clever as a smartphone.)

"Sorry . . . can't . . . breathe," I said. Which was a way to delay telling her the truth, but it also *was* the truth.

"Hmmm . . ." she said. "I'll just ask Thor."

“Gasp,” I replied, which was not only an expression of horror, but also an intense need for oxygen.

Sif sprinted ahead to ask Thor for the truth.

TURDS.

A few minutes later, both Sif and Thor slowed down and ran in step with me.

“So, you ignored my plan and went with yours,” hissed Sif. “And got Thor captured. Then got yourself captured. Typical.”

In my head I was screaming, “I CAN EXPLAIN!” but I couldn’t even make a gasping noise out loud. My lungs burned like the fiery depths of Muspelheim.

At that point, Sif decided we were safe to slow down to a walk—or, in my case, a stagger.

When I could breathe and speak again—about ten minutes later—I explained that, yes, I had ignored Sif’s plan and got Thor captured, but I had meant to fix it all. “I’m sorry I didn’t fix it before you noticed,” I apologized, which I think was very big of me.

Sif glared at me. “You can’t just do something bad and expect no consequences so long as you cover it up!”

“But I *have* had consequences,” I pointed out.

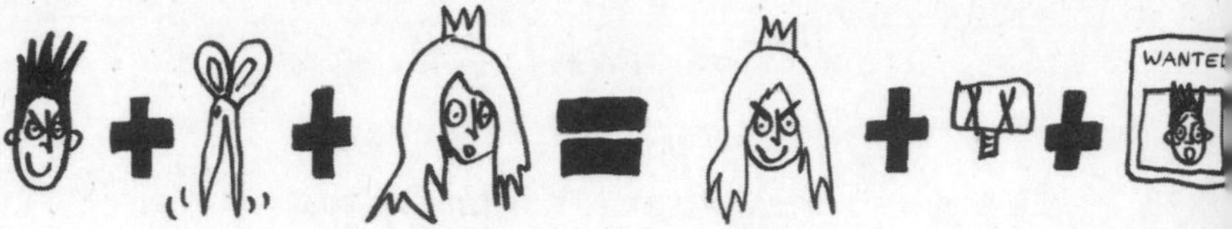

“So now we’re even!” I said.

Sif sighed from the bottom of her powerful lungs. All around us, the grass wilted for a moment. “That is *not* how this works! It’s not like . . . arithmetic. Can’t you behave like other people’s feelings matter for one minute?”

I frowned. “Why should I?”

After all, my feelings are the important feelings. Everything else is just . . . well, not my concern.

Sif gave me a look of pure rage and all the grass around us withered to brown. “I wish I’d just *hit* you with Thor’s hammer instead of framing you for stealing it. No wonder everybody hates you! You’re impossible to like! Or even talk to!”

Ointment I need for that BURN

Well, that hurt a little, I have to confess.

“Can you stop talking about feelings?” moaned Thor. “It makes my head hurt.”

The rest of the trudge home was in awkward silence, broken by occasional loud grunts from Thor.

When we got in, Hyrrokkin and Heimdall were waiting for us. Thor told them what had happened, and the next hour went something like this:

Just as the yelling from Hyrrokkin and Heimdall finished, when Sif was about to start a whole new round of yelling, the doorbell rang.

"THANK YOU, ODIN!" I cried, and rushed to answer it.

To my surprise, Valerie and Georgina were standing on the doorstep. Valerie was looking worried. Georgina was looking confused and a bit angry. I hate it when people look like that because they're usually about to shout at me.

"Something happened," said Valerie. "I"—she glanced at Georgina—"don't know what I'm allowed to say."

Well, that was intriguing. And, bonus, involved no shouting. I invited them in to share my infinite wisdom.

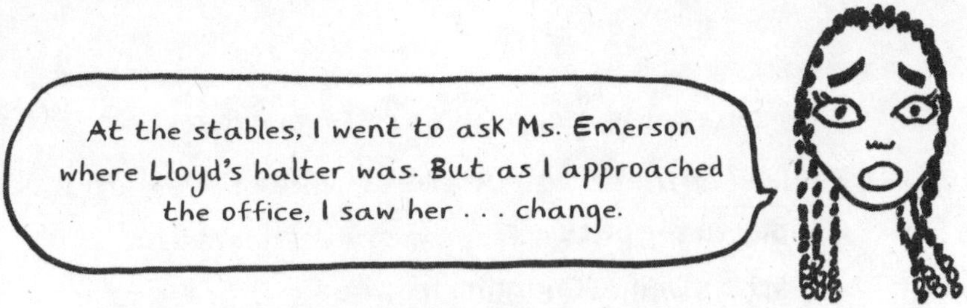

At the stables, I went to ask Ms. Emerson where Lloyd's halter was. But as I approached the office, I saw her . . . change.

Change what? Her socks? The clocks? The political system of this measly mortal country? I couldn't believe she was doing a dramatic pause. That's *my* trick!

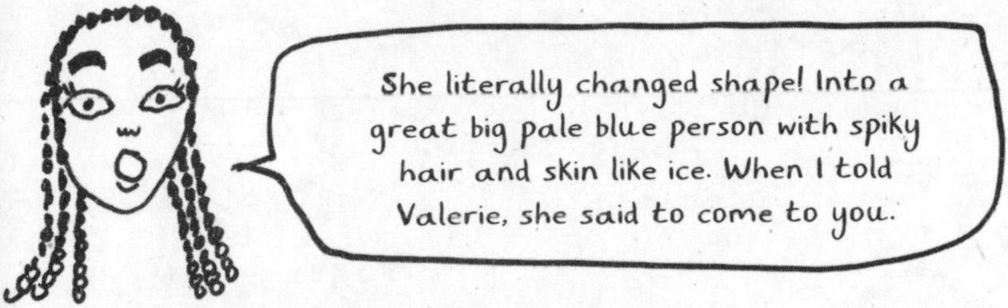

She literally changed shape! Into a great big pale blue person with spiky hair and skin like ice. When I told Valerie, she said to come to you.

"I couldn't break my oath," Valerie said to me in a whisper. Then she added, more loudly, "But, Georgina, I really want to tell you everything." She turned to me. "So . . . what can I say?"

"Er . . . pass." I turned to Hyrrokkin and Heimdall. "Mom? Dad?"

Hyrrokkin and Heimdall looked around for someone to whom they could pass the buck. But their only options were Fido (a dog) and Thor (well, he's Thor), so they kept the buck, reluctantly.

After a pause, Heimdall said, "Given what she's seen already, I believe Odin would understand if we completed the picture."

"Who's Odin?" Georgina frowned.

"His boss." Hyrrokin pointed at Heimdall.

"The Allfather," said Thor.

"The greatest of the Aesir," said Sif.

"Ruler of Asgard, father of wisdom, quester after knowledge . . ." added Heimdall unhelpfully.

I held up a hand.

They were doing a terrible job of explaining things.

"I believe I should take it from here."

So I did.

Georgina, I may appear to be an ordinary yet very handsome mortal...
but I am in fact a GOD!
A god?
A god!
Hmm.
LOL, OK.

Her face contained a distinct lack of wonder and even less awe. How rude! Unless perhaps that *is* her awe face but she's bad at facial expressions?

"And what was the thing I saw at the stables?" she asked.

"She was a Frost Giant. They are the enemies of the gods," I said.

Then I launched into a beautifully told description of the nature of gods and giants.

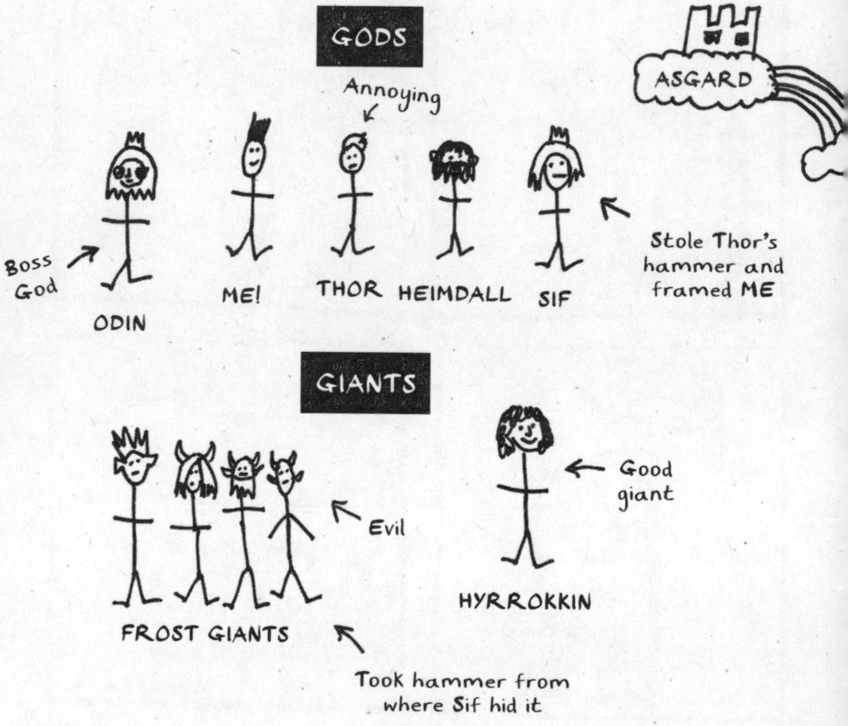

When I'd finished, Georgina sat in contemplation for a moment. Then she said, "You're seriously saying you are a god?"

"I know this information about the nature of the universe may be a shock to you—" I began, but she cut me off.

"No, I mean . . . *you*. A god? Him, I could believe," she said, gesturing at Thor. "And her," she added, indicating Sif. "But you? You're so . . . rude. And petty. When you accused me of stealing some hammer, I thought you were just a jealous boy with problems."

She turned to me with fury in her eyes.

What are you the god of? Being a jerk?
I'm the god of chaos, mischief, and trickery!
That's just "being a jerk" in fancy words.

"I believe we are getting somewhat off topic," I said with a cough. Since she'd just called me petty, I had to prove her wrong, so I could not rise to the insult. "We should focus on the fact that evil Frost

Giants have Thor's mighty hammer, and we should start by asking why they wanted to steal the hammer in the first place. And why—"

I stopped mid-flow.

"What is it?" asked Valerie.

"Perhaps he has indigestion?" said Thor. "That can sometimes make you cease speaking in case you belch?"

"No! I stopped because something just occurred to me," I said. "Why did they want Thor *as well as* the hammer? They clearly didn't want to kill him, or they'd have done that as soon as they had him in their power."

Very maturely, I didn't turn to the others yelling, "I AM RIGHT. I WAS RIGHT. IN YOUR FACES, LOSERS!"

Everyone leaned in toward Thor.

"Did they ask you any questions while you were held captive?" asked Sif. "Secret codes to get into Asgard, anything like that?"

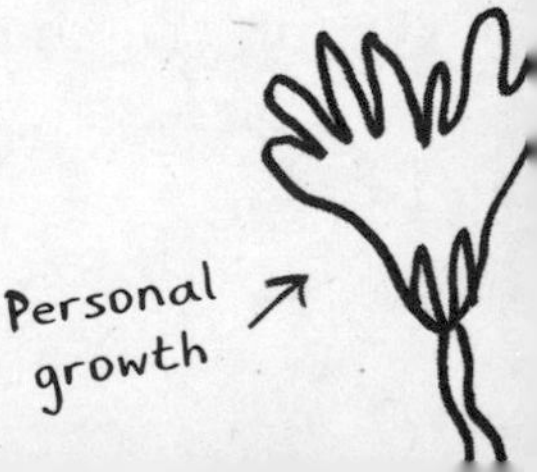

Ha! Like Thor would remember a secret code. His password on the school computers is **123Thor**. And that's only because the system wouldn't let him have **1234**.

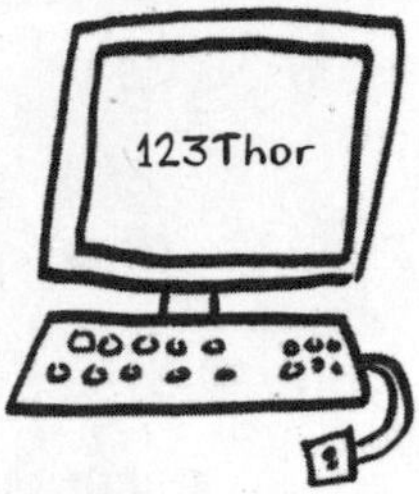

Thor shrugged. "They didn't ask me any questions."

"Maybe you rescued Thor and Loki before the giants had a chance to do whatever they had planned, Sif?" said Georgina. "It might've been something that needed to happen at a particular time. I dunno about all your god stuff but . . . like, sacrifice him at the full moon or something?"

"Thor, did they say *anything* that made you think they had something planned?" I asked. "Even a tiny detail might help us."

Thor racked his (very puny) brain. You could practically see the cogs of his mind whirring. All two of them.

"Well," he said at last. "They did take some of my blood."

I snorted so hard that the inside of my mortal nose nearly fell out. "And you didn't think that was worth mentioning?"

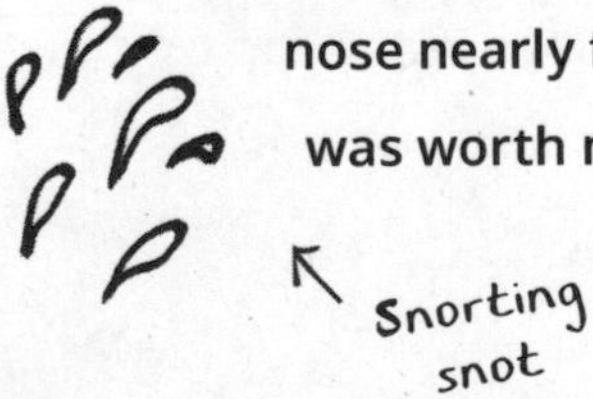

Thor waved his hand. "I just assumed they wanted to drink the blood of their enemies. Frost Giants do that sort of thing."

I put my head in my hands. I despaired! Luckily, Valerie had something sensible to say.

"So, they've got Thor's hammer and his blood. What would they do with them?" she asked. My friend, who has clearly wholly forgiven me for accusing Georgina of stealing the hammer, even if I didn't need forgiving.

I remembered something and took Hyrrokkin's spell book down from the bookshelf. It was *heavy*. Giants do *not* design books for mortal boys who are puny of arm.

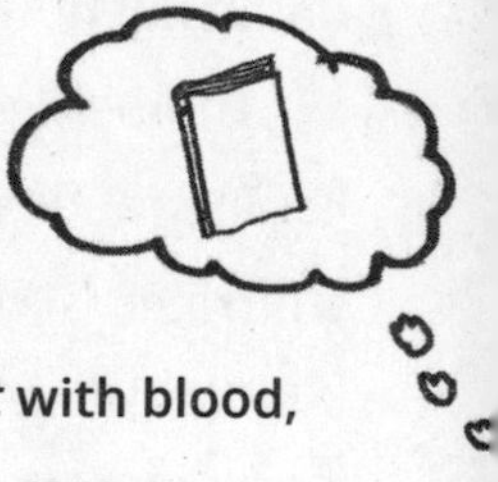

"It sounds like they're planning a spell to me," I said, flipping through the pages to find anything involving blood and/or hammers. There were a *lot* with blood, but hammer spells were, helpfully, quite rare. Narrowing it down to one spell depended on the third ingredient, which we didn't know. But it had to be one of these:

Conditions for each of these spells vary depending on the season and the target of the spell

magic hammer + blood of the owner + a baby's fingernail = a curse of eternal pain

magic hammer + blood of the owner + a raven's feather = a spell to make you the wisest in all the worlds for a day

magic hammer + blood of the owner + mistletoe = a magical explosion of enormous power

I realized that the answer had been right in front of me. Or rather, hanging over my head.

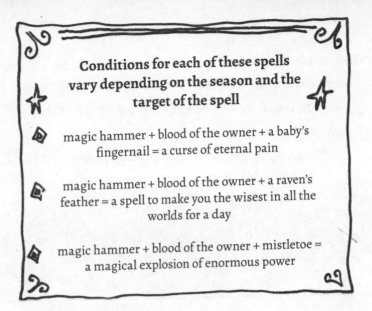

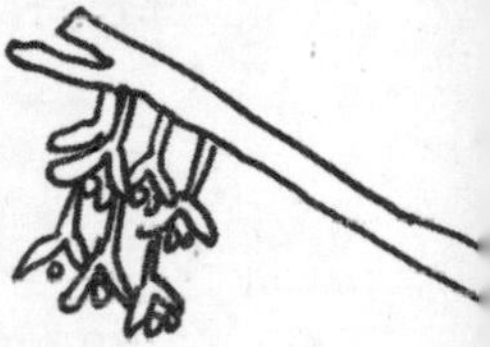

"MISTLETOE!"

"What?" asked Georgina.

"That's the final ingredient!" I said, astounded at my own genius. "I saw one of the people at the stables gathering mistletoe when I came to see Valerie. I thought they were treating a powerful magical ingredient as a weed, but they weren't! They were a giant in disguise gathering it for a spell!"

All eyes were on me. The world felt good again.

Then I had a horrible realization. The stables

were right next to the start of the rainbow bridge. The way home to Asgard. The spell was a powerful magical explosive . . .

"They're going to blow up the bridge to Asgard!" I said.

But I couldn't enjoy their adoration due to my state of extreme terror.

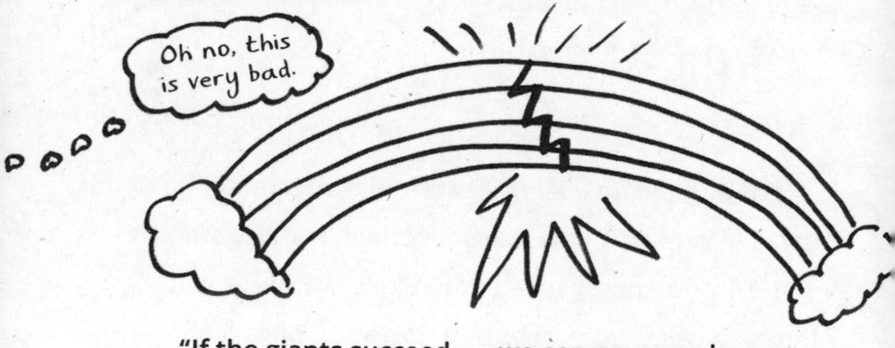

"If the giants succeed . . . we can never go home again," I said.

"It also means the other gods can't come here," said Sif. "So we're all alone. Without Thor's hammer, it would be just a small band of gods against all the Frost Giants of Jotunheim."

For once, I agreed with Georgina.

Valerie turned to her. "You don't have to be a part of this," she said. "This isn't your mess."

"Are you kidding?" said Georgina, pointing at me.

"Do you think I'm going to leave it to that guy to save the world?"

After another hour, a lot of bickering, and several plates of snacks brought in by Heimdall, we agreed on a plan.

Given Thor's rather hostile demeanor, I decided to save that tale for another day.

Besides, it was getting late.

I yawned, which set Thor off yawning, followed by Valerie and Georgina and Sif. Mortals have many contagious diseases, and yawning is one of them. (I do believe that if a mortal ever gets their hands on this diary, they will start yawning as they read this page.)

"We may be mighty gods," I said, "but I'm in the body of an eleven-year-old boy who slept on the floor of an abandoned cottage last night. And I am POOPED. Let the plan commence tomorrow with fresh eyes. And perhaps a fresher smell," I added, sniffing at Thor.

"But I am NOT tired!" said Thor, smelling his own armpit and wincing.

"In any case," I added, yawning, "we need to spy on the giants to find out the timing of the spell. And they'll be asleep tonight. So unless you want to spy on them snoring, we can wait until tomorrow!"

Thor grumpily (and stinkily) agreed.

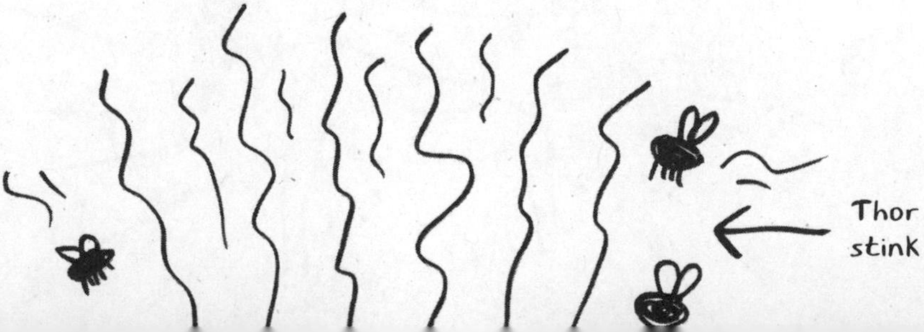

Day Twenty-One

Sunday

LOKI VIRTUE SCORE OR LVS:

-1600

Plus 1000 points for ACTUALLY DOING YOUR JOB for once

! I CAN take points off for excessive smugness, you know . . .

After breakfast, I flew to the stables in the form of a bird and through the window to join the other horses. Then I adopted my cunning disguise.

Soon, a pair of giants came in with refreshments for the horses. They clearly did not bother with mortal disguises when they were alone.

Or when they think they're alone, mwahahahaha!

Horse food is surprisingly delicious when you're a horse. As they fed us, they chatted. They said nothing of value for at least ten minutes. But on the plus side, I was able to do a big horse poop on General Glacier's boot while I waited.

Finally, the giants said something interesting . . . and horrific.

"How many mortals do you think you'll keep alive as pets, once we rule this realm?" Captain Icebeard asked the general.

She thought about this. “Oh, maybe a dozen,” she said. “We’ll assign a heated room in the palace. They will not survive otherwise.”

Icebeard nodded and gave a blissful smile. “Just think . . . eternal winter. And the only animals remaining will be those hardy enough to survive the extreme cold. A culling of the weak!” he said approvingly.

I pictured a world of eternal ice and snow—and mass extinction of all but the hardiest arctic animals.

On the plus side, Arctic foxes *are* very cute.

But the downside is . . . everything and everyone else would be dead.

Including Valerie.

I stopped chewing my pony feed in alarm, wishing I could get out of there immediately to warn the others.

But I still didn't know *when* this icy disaster would occur. Glacier and Icebeard left, but the more junior Frost Giants—Corporal Coldnose and Sergeant McFreezy—came in to muck out the stables. Apparently no child labor was available that day.

Now, the thing I really love about Frost Giants is how much they like to complain.

When they'd finished whining about the lack of feasting while they were on a mission on Earth, and about the Frost Giant King, and about the hot weather on Midgard, we hit the jackpot!

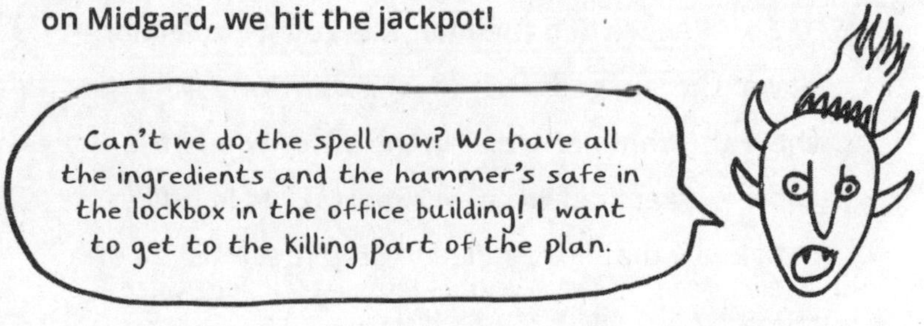

Can't we do the spell now? We have all the ingredients and the hammer's safe in the lockbox in the office building! I want to get to the killing part of the plan.

I couldn't help but feel that this giant was a soul twin for Thor.

The other giant shook his head. "We cannot do it yet. The general said that the risen moon on the next day of the sun goddess would give us the conditions we need for the spell to work upon Bifrost in this season. But then, we're good to go."

"Next step, complete world dominance!" said Sergeant McFreezy. "Or is it domination?"

"Who cares? We won't need to use mortal language then. Plus we never have to endure those stupid bodies ever again," said Corporal Coldnose. "They're so hot and sweaty and puny."

"Did you know, mortals can get mushrooms growing on their feet?"

"Disgusting. Good thing we'll be wiping most of humanity out," said Corporal Coldnose.

So, I knew when the plan was going into action—"day of the sun goddess" must mean Sunday. I knew where the hammer was—in the office where the stable workers did whatever mortals do in offices. And I knew that if we failed to stop it, almost all of humanity would be wiped out.

So, no pressure then.

As soon as it was safe, I trotted out of the stable and transformed into my mortal form. Then I met the others at the park and brought them up to speed.

I didn't feel ready for that. I was terrified. Valerie put a hand on my shoulder.

"It's OK," said Valerie. "We can stop them together. As a team."

Georgina laughed. "When we became friends, I did not see us preventing the Apocalypse."

"We haven't prevented it yet," said Thor grimly.

"Captain Happypants here is ever the optimist."

"I don't like plans that don't involve hitting things with hammers."

"Well, it's a good thing you've got me here to plan for you," I said. Then I looked around at Sif and Georgina and Valerie, feeling a certain unfamiliar warmth in the chest region. "Or rather . . . you've got all of us."

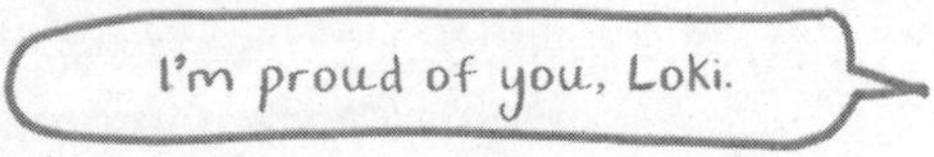

Don't get carried away. I just like the sound of my own voice motivating my witless troops.

Day Twenty-Two

Monday

LOKI VIRTUE SCORE OR LVS:

-500

Points gained for being a team player. I'm impressed. This is an unusual feeling for me.

After discovering that the world might end next Sunday, going back to school was a bit of an anti-climax. But Heimdall said that the end of the world was no excuse to let my studies slide. He said some other things, too, but I forgot to listen.

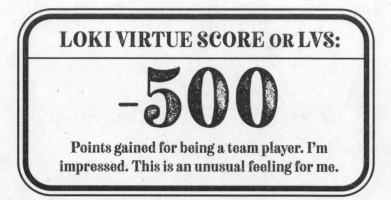

Blah blah waffle stuff scolding.

In art class, I found myself idly doodling Thor's hammer. It was an excellent likeness. Which gave me an idea . . . I went to find Sif on the playground.

"Sif, I have a mission for you," I said. "I have an idea for how to stop the spell from working."

She looked skeptical, but when I told her my plan, she smiled. "Easy-peasy. But it might take a few days. I'll leave right away."

"Just make sure you're back before Sunday," I said.

And, Diary, I'm not writing down what plan Sif was off to put into motion, because that's the kind of suspense-creating god I am.

You'll have to tell me eventually though. Those are the rules set down by Odin. In the end, you will tell me, or you will face the consequences! !

Yes, in the end, I will tell you. That's how suspense works! Honestly, for a diary alleged to contain the wisdom of Odin, he didn't program you very well when it comes to narrative devices.

Odin cares not for narrative devices! !

I know. I've had to sit through many of his speeches in Asgard . . .

Sif left after break, pausing on her way out to tell

the teacher she was feeling unwell, then sneaking off to make a quick phone call a little while later.

Sarah's mom here. She's home now, but there's a lot of snot and vomit, so I suspect she'll be out of school for a few days.
Please take the plague child far away!

At least it probably went something like that.

I told the others about the Sif plan as soon as I could. Including the part where [redacted] and [redacted]—oh, and the really exciting bit where [redacted]

! **You're really *not* going to even give me a hint, are you?**

Nope.

Day Twenty-Three

Tuesday

LOKI VIRTUE SCORE OR LVS:

–550

50 points lost for insulting Odin's speeches

No Sif. Of course. She *did* say the plan might take a few days.

Day Twenty-Four

Wednesday

LOKI VIRTUE SCORE OR LVS:

-550

Holding steady. The calm before the storm perhaps.

Still no Sif. How many days *is* a "few" exactly? Three?

Day Twenty-Five

Thursday

LOKI VIRTUE SCORE OR LVS:

-550

Same . . .

Could a "few" mean four?

Not that I'm worried about Sif. I'm worried about our plan.

But the journey she's going on could be dangerous. What if she meets a dragon along the way? That might be really dangerous for . . . our plan.

Day Twenty-Six

Friday

LOKI VIRTUE SCORE OR LVS:

-550

Remains steady. Though I might give you a few points if you tell me where Sif is. The suspense is killing me . . .

Still no Sif. I don't like this. What could have happened to her? If she's been eaten by a dragon, I'm going to have to come up with a new plan.

Not that I have any problem coming up with plans. I'm a genius! But . . . I liked that plan. I'm oddly attached to that plan. I'm worried about that plan. She . . . I mean, it . . . was really growing on me.

! Did you just . . . express concern for Sif?

What? No! Never! Not Loki! Loki shows no concern for his sworn enemies!

Anyway, I texted Valerie lots after school in case she's nervous about our plan. She pretended to be fine and even told me to stop worrying—when I was the one calming her down! The nerve!

I told Hyrrokkin about our plan, and how worried I was about our plan, and she said that she had something fun scheduled to take our minds off waiting tomorrow. I hope it doesn't involve character-building craft activities. Hyrrokkin has some wild ideas of what counts as "fun."

See you later, I'm off to my meat-sculpting class.

Day Twenty-Seven

Saturday

LOKI VIRTUE SCORE OR LVS:

-450

100 points for caring about Sif, even if you won't admit it

Still no Sif. Tomorrow is the day. Fingers crossed Sif ~~comes back safely~~ brings us what we need for a successful plan.

! Please. I can read the crossed-out part perfectly clearly. Don't insult my intelligence. I KNOW you are talking about Sif. You're worried about her. You care about her as a person.

No I do not! She's basically my nemesis! She set me up for a crime I didn't commit!

Only because of all the ones you *did* commit. !

Anyway . . . Hyrrokkin's surprise involved piling us into a rental van because our car was too small. She'd invited Valerie and Georgina, too. Heimdall was already sitting in the driver's seat with a "World's Best Driver" hat on.

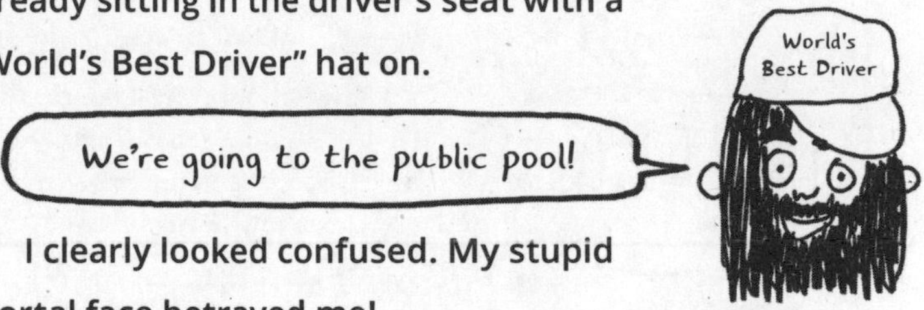

I clearly looked confused. My stupid mortal face betrayed me!

"You'll love it," said Georgina. "It's so much fun!"

"Is there violence?" asked Thor.

"Not usually," said Georgina. "But with all of you, who knows?"

"You must promise *not* to commit acts of violence at the pool, or I will turn this van around!" said Heimdall.

We all promised not to do that, and Heimdall seemed satisfied.

On the way, we performed a mortal ritual called the sing-along.

Sing-along: when a group of mortals all sing together, badly, often in a vehicle or clustered around a broken piano. The ritual requires this singing to be out of tune as well as out of time and preferably also includes a lot of the wrong lyrics. The ritual becomes extra powerful if those lyrics are rude.

The wheels on the poop are round and brown! Round and brown, round and brown!

When we first arrived at the pool, I did not love it. I was expected to enter the changing rooms and emerge wearing nothing but a very small pair of waterproof underpants. The indignity!

But things improved somewhat when I discovered the possibilities of this new trickster playground.

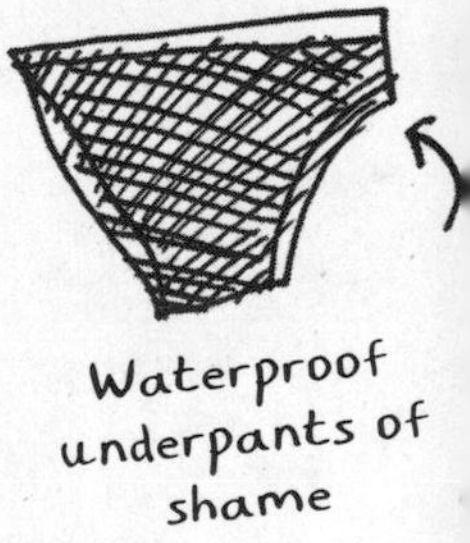

However, what was *less* pleasant was the feeling of my eyes being on fire when I opened them underwater. I thought perhaps I was being attacked by some kind of poisonous underwater beast.

It turns out that mortals put a horrible chemical into swimming water. I later looked up why they would do a thing like that, and the answer was even less pleasant.

Search
WHY DO PEOPLE PUT CHLORINE IN POOLS?

Let's just say, human beings are disgusting—and leave it at that.

Thankfully, there were showers, so I was able to wash the chlorine—and Odin knows what else—off my skin. When everyone was dressed, we went and ate lunch at the café. I looked around at my friends, my former enemy Georgina, and my fake family, and I gave a little sigh. I thought about the swimming pool and its highly enjoyable slides freezing over under the dominion of the Frost Giants. I thought of my friends as prisoners . . . or worse. "Earth *is* worth protecting, after all," I said, biting into a french fry.

"You're so weird," said Georgina.

"For that, I am stealing one of your fries," I said, and did so.

This started a fry war that escalated quickly into a food fight, which led to us being banned for life.

So, in the end, we *did* carry out acts of violence at the public pool. And it wasn't even Thor's fault!

Day Twenty-Eight

Sunday

LOKI VIRTUE SCORE OR LVS:

-500

50 points lost for getting banned from the public pool. It would have been more, but in this case it wasn't ENTIRELY your fault.

Sif *still* wasn't back when I woke up. I decided to check her hotel room just in case.

When I got upstairs, there was no sign of Sif. But I did check that the jacuzzi was working for when she got back. I'm kind like that. And I helped out by eating the things from the tiny fridge in her room, because she clearly didn't like them—they were untouched.

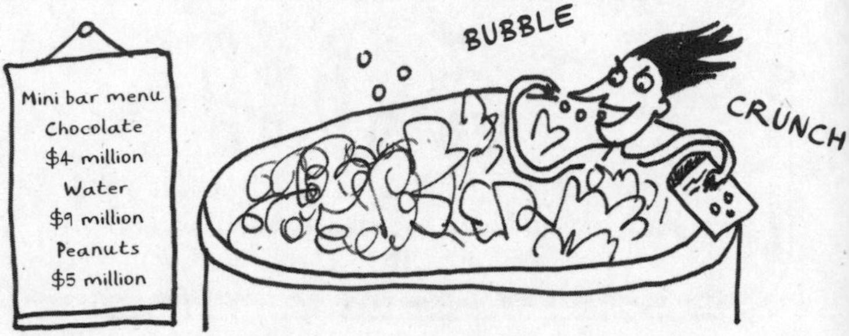

Time for plan B: Create a distraction.

When I got back from the hotel, I gathered Thor, Georgina, and Valerie to hash out the details.

There was only a small window for the spell: exactly when the moon rises and the wind blows and the birds sing. We just needed to occupy the giants for long enough to prevent them from casting the spell.

Georgina and Valerie suggested setting a horse loose so the giants would have to catch it. I pointed out that the giants would probably just . . . not catch it. They don't care about the horses.

Wow, they really ARE evil!

"You could turn *us* into animals and we could charge?" said Valerie. "That would distract them!"

Everyone liked that idea. But which animal?

Valerie shook her head. "The answer is *obvious*," she said. "Horses!"

"Because it's a stable and we could sneak up on the giants before we charge at them?" asked Thor.

"Yes. But also because it would be *so awesome to be a horse*!" Valerie almost yelled.

We're going to be horses!
HORSES!

Eventually, evening came. Before we went, Hyrrokkin and Heimdall made us dinner. “You can’t save the world on an empty stomach,” pointed out Heimdall.

Hopefully it wasn’t my last meal on Earth, because it was dreadful.

! Lie detected. You had seconds.

They were *pity* seconds. I didn’t want Heimdall to feel bad. I’m a Good God™ now, remember?

! Hmmmmm.

After dinner we walked slowly to the stables. I hoped that Sif would appear suddenly.

She did not.

Now, as I’ve said before, the rainbow bridge appears on the sidewalk right outside the stables when it’s conjured.

As long as we could keep the giants away from that spot until the moon was fully risen, we'd be OK.

The stable yard was dark and quiet, except for a light on in a room that Valerie explained was called the tack room. Voices were coming from within. That must be where the giants were.

We assembled in our human forms, then I transformed us, one by one, into horses.

The moon was rising. It was time. I gave the signal, and the horses charged.

It was beautiful!
stirring music

It was chaos (YAY!)
me, supervising from a safe distance.
CRACKLE
CRACKLE
Fire?
SNORT
KICK

Retreat!
EEK!
Soon . . .
They have us surrounded.
CRACKLE
SNORT
Hmm.
1 . . . 2 . . . 3
REHUMANIZE
Where's General Glacier?

General Glacier must have gone to get the hammer to start the spell. Our distraction hadn't worked on her! CURSES!

"Thor!" I yelled. "General Glacier's gone for the hammer in the office! Go after her!"

"I need my true form!" yelled Thor.

So I turned him into a god—not a boy—and he roared, chasing after the leader of the Frost Giants.

"Someone's coming from behind that stable block," whinnied Georgina. I turned her into her human form so she could sneak up on them. (Hooves are LOUD.)

As Georgina ran to check the stables, I saw Valerie transform, ensnared by a Frost Giant's magical chains.

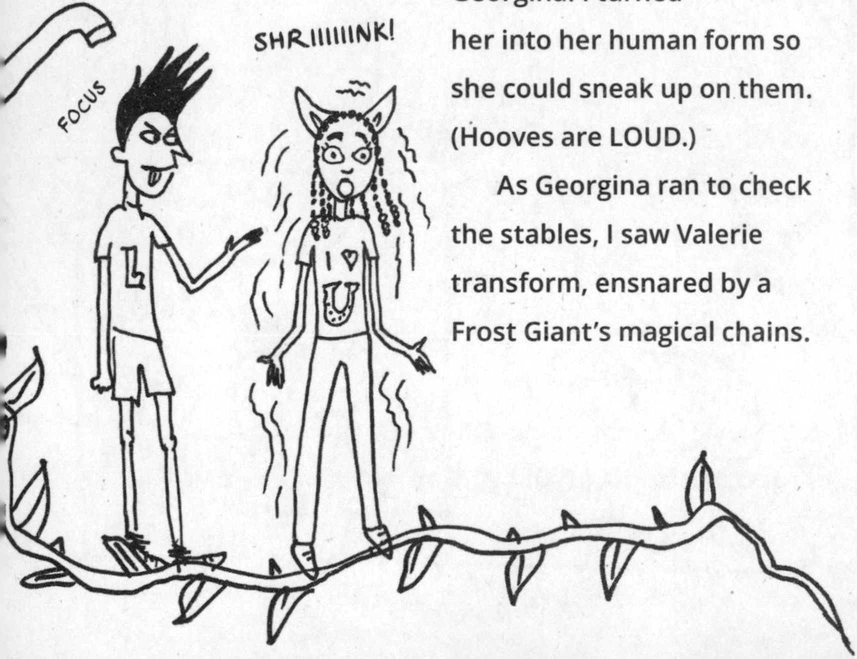

Forgetting the danger posed to my puny mortal form, I ran toward her, not noticing a Frost Giant waiting to grab me by the scruff of the neck.

Moments later, Valerie and I were flung into a stall, and the door was locked behind us.

"We'll deal with you later," growled Captain Icebeard. Valerie and I ran to the window, but Georgina was nowhere to be seen. So it was four giants against Thor. Without his hammer. It was hopeless—even in his divine form.

Lightning crackled overhead, so he was clearly trying his best. But I had the terrible feeling that there was no way out. The giants would cast their spell. The bridge would be broken. And the world would be theirs.

Except . . .

"Valerie," I hissed. "I have a way out!"

She looked at me expectantly.

"They'll have to summon the rainbow bridge in order to destroy it," I said. "There'll be a moment when we can cross it, before the destruction begins. We just need to get out of here."

No, we can't.
What do you mean?

"We can't leave. What about the others?" she said.

I was annoyed! She was ruining my heroic rescue! "What about them?"

Valerie pulled her hand away. "I'm not leaving Georgina behind. I'm not leaving"—she looked out the window—"my moms. Rusty! The horses! Everyone on this planet!"

"But it's the only way," I said. Why didn't she understand? I was doing a good thing! I was saving her from the Apocalypse!

She shook her head. "Loki, don't you care about anyone else but yourself?"

"I care about you, clearly, for I am going to save you from the end of the world!" I objected.

"What about Sif? You were worried about her

all week. Don't you care about her? And what about Thor? Don't you care about him?"

The words "No, obviously not. I hate Thor!" were about to form on my lips, when there was a shout from outside.

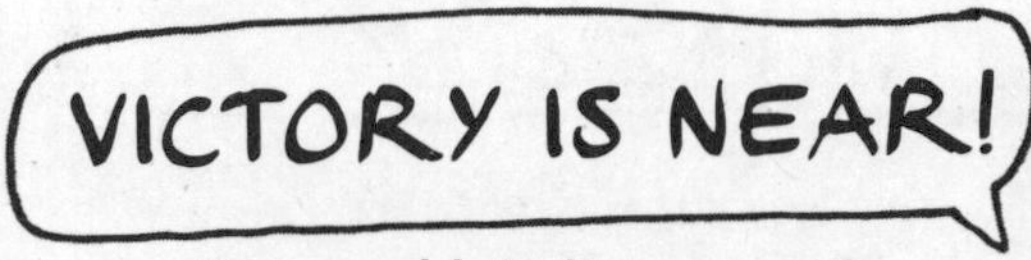

"You couldn't distract us for long, fools," said General Glacier. "The thunder god is contained. Come, comrades! Bring the ingredients!"

The other giants brought a heap of dried, ground plant matter and a vial of red liquid. The mistletoe and Thor's blood. General Glacier handed off Thor's chain to Captain Icebeard, who tugged a growling Thor to one side.

General Glacier began to crumble mistletoe onto the sidewalk beside the hammer and spoke the words of the spell.

"And now the blood," cried General Glacier.

She held up the vial of blood, and the giants continued chanting. From what I'd read in Hyrrokkin's book, the chanting wasn't a necessary part of the spell; giants just like a nice chant.

I mean, who doesn't?

The rainbow bridge grew brighter and brighter. I could see that it was solid now. Our glittering way out. A multicolored path to freedom and joy and safety, not to mention really, really comfortable beds and amazing food.

This was our chance. I was looking at Thor, who was grim-faced and struggling with his chains, unable to use his powers. Fear flashed in his eyes. This shook me. Thor wasn't supposed to get scared!

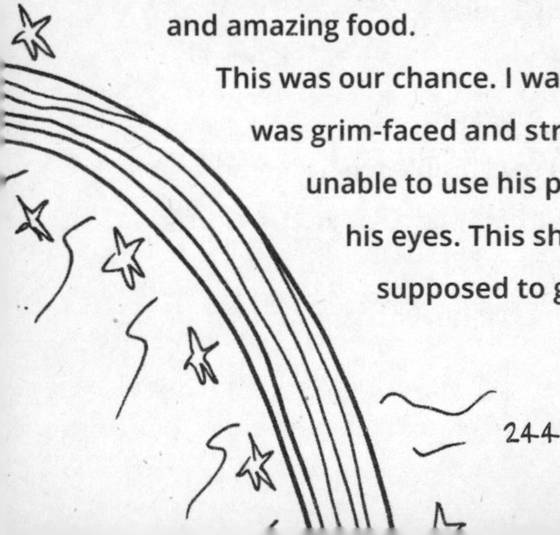

But if Thor was scared, all the more reason to run away. All I had to do was turn Valerie into something portable and rush up the rainbow bridge to safety. This was the moment to do it.

So why wasn't I escaping? Something felt . . . wrong.

I groaned. Before I was a Good God™, I'd just do whatever I felt like doing. But now, I heard that annoying little voice in my head . . .

> Could it be that you're not escaping because you don't want to leave? That you truly care about Thor and don't want him to be hurt? Maybe you harbor warm feelings for Sif, even if you don't like her?

That's definitely not it, I thought. I don't care about Thor. He's just annoyed me for millennia, so I'm rather used to him. And Sif? Sif is my nemesis! That's like an enemy but worse!

> Then think. Think of the world itself. All its beauty, all the things humans have made and done. Imagine all that being frozen forever, destroyed under a blanket of ice.

Oh. Now that blow landed. If I left this place behind to shrivel and freeze, I'd never again watch a

TV show in which mortals engaged in humiliating yet amusing competitions. And worse. I'd never taste another potato chip again! Never feel my tongue caressed by the chemical tang of chili beef or vinegar and anchovy! In that moment, I decided. I was going to save the world.

"Valerie," I said. "I'm staying."

"For Thor and your family?" she asked, looking thrilled.

"FOR CHIPS!" I declared.

Her face fell for some reason, but before she could applaud my virtuous decision, I realized I knew how I could stop the spell. Perhaps. Time for a little trickster transformation!

I zipped out of the mesh window, making a beeline—or rather a waspline—for General Glacier.

But I was too late. As I reached her, my stinger poised, she was already pouring the dark liquid onto the handle of the hammer.

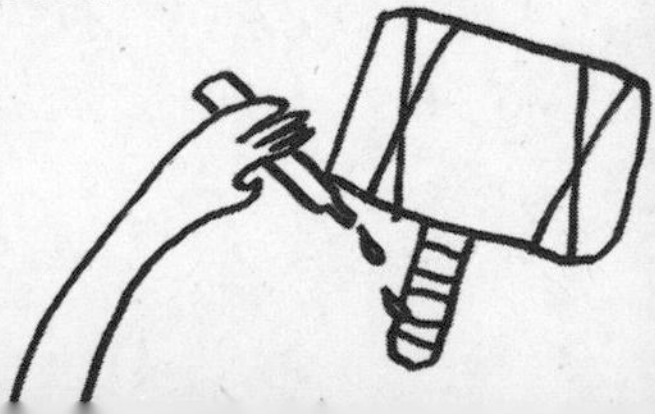

This was the final step of the spell. This would unlock the hammer's power and create an explosion so mighty it would break the rainbow bridge.

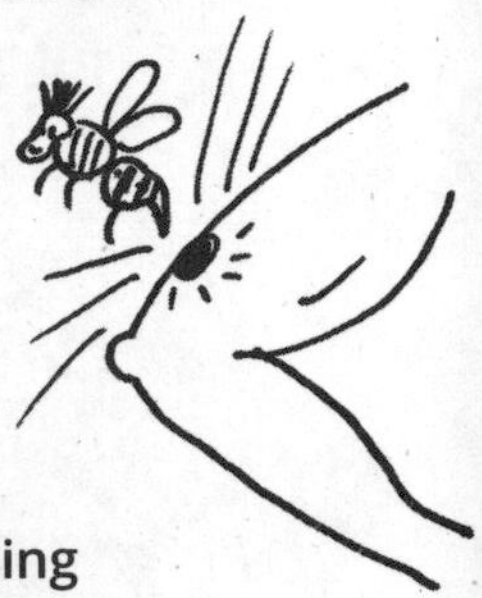

Thor howled with rage and fear.

I swept in and stung the general on the arm. (Just because the giants had won didn't mean she couldn't be sore in her victory.)

She swatted me away and I fell, transforming into my boy form before I hit the ground. I staggered to my feet and saw Valerie's pale face at the window of the stable.

The giants stepped back, awaiting the tremendous blast that would cut the gods off from Midgard forever and leave them to rule and ruin the world.

And . . .

The bridge stayed there in the sky, as sparkly and multicolored as ever.

The hammer sat there doing nothing.

What was happening?

Then a thought of pure impossible joy bubbled up. Did Sif . . . ? Did she . . . ?

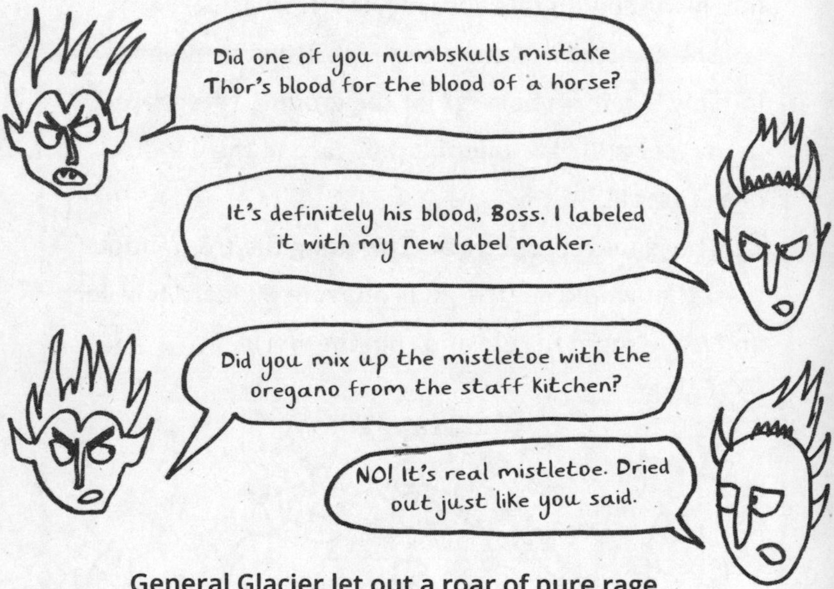

Did one of you numbskulls mistake Thor's blood for the blood of a horse?
It's definitely his blood, Boss. I labeled it with my new label maker.
Did you mix up the mistletoe with the oregano from the staff kitchen?
NO! It's real mistletoe. Dried out just like you said.

General Glacier let out a roar of pure rage.

At that moment, I realized Valerie was by my side. "That door had a *terrible* lock," she said, waving a bobby pin at me. (Who needs Odin's skeleton key?) "But I don't understand. What went wrong with the spell?"

Just then, Sif and Georgina emerged from behind one of the stables. Sif was carrying something.

A hammer-shaped something.

Before the giants could register what was happening, Sif had unlocked Thor's chains and handed him the something.

"Yours, I believe?" she said.

I stood with Sif, Valerie, and Georgina by my side, watching Thor fight the giants. We were bathed in the light of the rainbow bridge until it faded into the sky.

"Should we help?" asked Valerie, as Thor was thrown into the air.

"Nah, he's fine," said Sif. "Not sure the giants are though." We watched as Captain Icebeard sailed through the air and crumpled into a stable wall. He sank down to the ground, groaning.

I looked at Sif. "You did it," I said. "I'm impressed."

"Of course I did," said Sif. "I'm the greatest."

(Debatable.)

"Admittedly, I had help," said Sif. She gestured to Georgina.

"I distracted General Glacier while Sif did the switch," said Georgina.

"Ooh, how?" I asked.

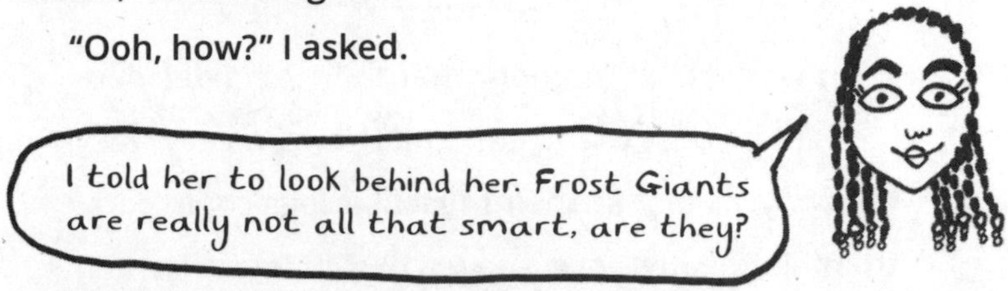

I told her to look behind her. Frost Giants are really not all that smart, are they?

"And Loki had a backup plan," added Valerie. "In case the hammer thing didn't work."

I felt a cold creep over me. Was she going to reveal my plan to flee? Everyone would know that I was a coward and a wretch.

Valerie went on, "He turned into a wasp to slow General Glacier so she wouldn't finish the spell."

"I was too late though," I pointed out.

But Valerie leaned closer and whispered, "You stayed. You did the right thing."

Then I heard another voice.

You did OK, Loki. I can't say you acted for the right reasons . . . but you did the right thing.

My conscience wasn't usually so nice to me. I could get used to this.

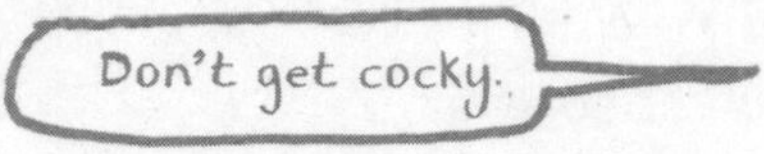

It was at that moment that the giants decided it might be best to retreat, and they ran very, very far away, as fast as their muscular legs could carry them. In the distance, I saw a blur of white ice stretching into the sky. The bridge to Jotunheim!

Thor returned to us, brandishing his hammer.

There is no joy so pure as the joy of battle. But I could have gone another few rounds . . . spoilsport giants.

As the icy bridge faded into the sky, I turned to Sif. "So, what took you so long?"

"You know how you said I could just show up at the realm of dwarves and ask them to make me a replica of Thor's hammer for nothing?"

! Ah, so THAT'S what your secret plan was!

Sif folded her arms. "Well, they laughed in my face, asked if you'd put me up to such a ludicrous task, and demanded I do a quest before they'd make me a hammer."

"I got them to make a hammer for nothing before . . ." I said, surprised.

"And that's exactly why they said they wouldn't do anything without upfront payment." Sif shrugged. "It was quite fun, actually. Long story, involves a Valkyrie, a troll, and a fishing trip. I'll tell you sometime."

"I worry that you and Loki are more alike than I'd thought," said Thor, frowning. "Loki's always saying he'll tell me stories later. And he never does."

Just then, Heimdall and Hyrrokkin came thundering into the stables on the back of a wolf. Fido!

"If you're looking for the Frost Giants, they're gone," I said. "Thor beat them up with his hammer."

Snakes for reins,
usually kept in a
lass case at home.
TO WAR!

“Then they ran away,” said Thor, disappointed.

“What are you doing here?” I asked.

Heimdall and Hyrrokkin exchanged glances.

“We felt awful,” said Heimdall. “I’ve been so obsessed with forcing you to be independent that I haven’t been a supportive enough dad to you.”

“You’re not my dad,” I muttered.

“We came to help!” said Hyrrokkin. “But I’m so glad you’re all safe.”

“And we’re very proud of you,” said Heimdall. Then he did a very strange thing.

He hugged me.

I didn’t like it.

Well. I didn’t *hate* it.

It didn’t one hundred percent suck.

When the hug was over, I pushed him away.

Heimdall raised an eyebrow. “Home for a snack before bed?” he asked.

Day Twenty-Nine

Monday

LOKI VIRTUE SCORE OR LVS:

0

Many points gained for saving the world, even if your motivation was CHIPS

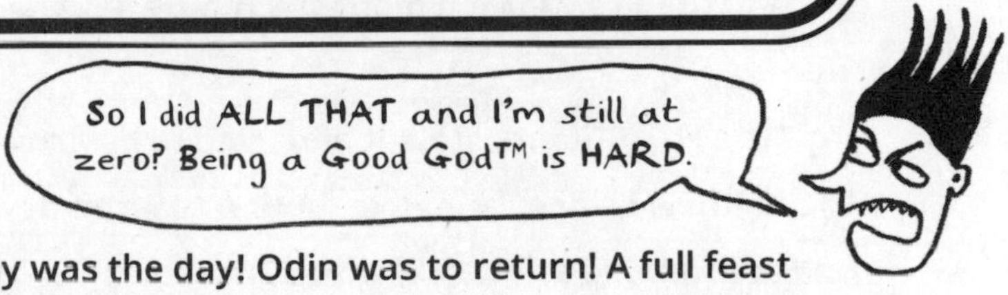

So I did ALL THAT and I'm still at zero? Being a Good God™ is HARD.

Today was the day! Odin was to return! A full feast cycle (or Three Beards, DST) had gone by since Odin departed on his wisdom quest. Ordinarily I wouldn't be thrilled about seeing Odin, but I had a victory to show off about this time—and a Sif to publicly embarrass. So, Sif came over before school and . . .

HEY, ODIN!

In an instant, Odin himself was standing there. Sif was quaking. Even Thor looked nervous.

Sif swallowed very hard.

"It's about Thor's hammer . . ." I began.

I could almost smell Sif's fear.

And then something made my mouth say these words.

"The Frost Giants stole it and tried to destroy the rainbow bridge, bringing about a Giantocracy on Earth as well as eternal winter. Don't worry: we got it back. It's all fine now. But I thought you should know."

Sif let out a long, slow breath.

"Interesting," said Odin. "Whose fault was it that the giants got hold of the hammer in the first place?"

I faltered. I had an opportunity for vengeance upon the one who falsely accused me of a crime! I could crow in victory and lord it over her.

"Didn't you read my out-of-Asgard message? I was on a wisdom quest, remember? I saw it in a vision!" Odin gave one of his annoyingly mysterious smiles.

That insufferable all-knowing turd burger!

He knew! All that worry about getting blamed for a crime I did not commit was for *nothing*!

Odin the Annoying turned to Sif. "So . . . what shall I do to one who framed a fellow god for a crime and almost allowed giants to destroy the rainbow bridge? Not to mention who also stole my skeleton key . . . Yes, I *did* notice that. What shall your punishment be?"

You could . . . let me off with a stern warning?

I pictured Sif in a dungeon full of snakes. It should have made me happy, but it didn't.

"Go easy on my wife," said Thor. "She only did it because Loki provoked her."

"Thor, if we all did bad things every time Loki provoked us, the gods would have brought about a thousand apocalypses by now," said Odin. He looked from Thor to Heimdall and Hyrrokkin and back to Thor. "So . . . what was *your* part in all this?"

I blamed Loki. I didn't trust him.
Same.

"While I consider how to punish Sif myself," said Odin, "perhaps Loki would like to choose a punishment of his own for her?"

A slow smile spread across my face.

"I'd like her to perform the song and dance she owes me," I said. "Now, please."

I think my favorite part was how much Odin laughed.

"Now, come, Sif," said Odin. "We shall return home, where you shall meet your punishment."

"Are you going to tell me what it is?" asked Sif.

"No," said Odin. "That's part of the punishment. But before you go, say sorry to Loki one more time."

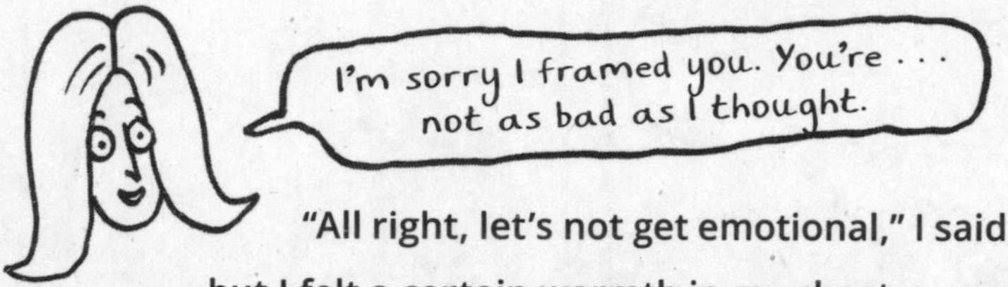

I'm sorry I framed you. You're . . . not as bad as I thought.

"All right, let's not get emotional," I said, but I felt a certain warmth in my chest area. Probably heartburn from last night's late snacking.

Then Sif and Odin vanished.

I thought after all that, maybe Thor and I would have a day off from school. But no. Life remains cruel. Heimdall said it was important to keep up our cover story *and* for me to work on my moral growth.

Rude.

At lunchtime Thor disappeared, leaving me to tell Valerie *all* about what had happened with Odin. Especially the song and dance. But also about how

Odin knew all along and still let it play out.

"He's not . . . watching us right now, is he?" said Valerie, glancing around her.

Mysterious old man . . . or Boss God Odin?

"Probably not. It's just when he drinks from Mimir's well, which gives you wisdom and insight, or asks Mimir direct questions. But he *does* go around in disguise, so who knows? He could be one of our teachers," I said.

We both shivered at that thought.

"That was good of you, not telling on Sif," said Valerie.

"Haven't you heard, I'm good now," I said.

"Sometimes," said Valerie. She nudged me with her shoulder.

I nudged her back. She nudged me harder, and I fell off the bench we were sitting on and onto the floor.

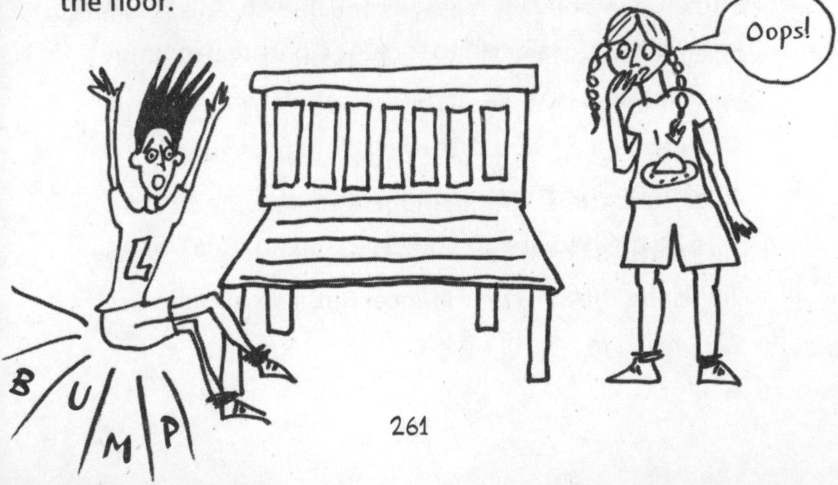
Oops!
BUMP

I sometimes forget how puny this mortal body is. Also, Valerie is *strong*. And my bum lacks padding.

"Sorry!" she said. She gave me a hand up.

"Take your pick," I said. "I'm sorry for asking you to run away and leave everyone behind. I'm sorry for thinking Georgina was the one who stole the hammer."

"And why *did* you do that?" asked Valerie.

"I was jealous. I thought she was going to take you away from me." I couldn't look her in the eye.

"That's . . . not how friendship works," said Valerie. "You can have more than one friend at the same time. I mean . . . this is the first time I've done it. But I always knew it was possible in theory. And perhaps in time you and Georgina could become good friends?"

"Perhaps," I said. "After all, I am incredibly charming, charismatic, and wonderful."

She pushed me off the bench again. But this time it was definitely on purpose.

Day Thirty

Tuesday

LOKI VIRTUE SCORE OR LVS:

-50

Points deducted for making Sif perform a humiliating song in front of everyone

Hey! She was fulfilling a blood oath!

School was uneventful, although I did learn how lakes are formed in geography class. I KNEW Odin was lying about that. He claimed lakes were made out of the blood of the primordial giant, Ymir. And he calls me a liar?

Now, now, the Allfather never said that was how it happened. The world's origins are shrouded in mystery. You're basing this on human versions of our lives, not Odin's words.

!

Well, he shouldn't have encouraged them! He should have corrected their nonsense!

> ! **It's not up to Odin to alter mortal texts. He's the Allfather, not an editor.**

Bah, I say. Bah. Anyway. Now I know the *truth*. So there.

As a treat for saving the world, Hyrrokkin and Heimdall took Valerie, Georgina, Thor, and me out for dinner at a restaurant where they serve deep-fried bird legs.

Enjoy my charred remains!
CHIK'N PALACE

We sat in a quiet corner of the restaurant, all jammed into a booth. I realized this meant I had a captive audience.

It was the *perfect* time for me to perform one of my very insulting poems.

Ten minutes later, I'd roasted almost every single person at the table and it was glorious.

When I had finished, Georgina leaned across the table. "That was funny," she said. "Mean, but funny. But . . . why didn't you do me?"

I shrugged. "After accusing you of a crime you didn't commit, I thought it might not be . . . well, what a good person would do."

Georgina shook her head. "Wrong. Friends don't leave friends out of mockery."

"Friends?" I said.

"On a trial basis," said Georgina.

"Would you like me to insult you now?"

"It's too late now," said Georgina. "You missed your chance. But don't worry. I'll be insulting *you* often."

She threw a french fry at me and I marveled at the idea that I might soon have not one but two friends. And not the kind of friends you have to force to come to a party under threat of violence. The kind that choose to be friends with you.

We all walked home, since that's where Valerie's and Georgina's parents were picking them up.

As we walked, Hyrrokkin pulled a package out of her bag and handed it to me. A gift! Though a disappointing one, as it appeared to be a book.

But then I opened it, and it was not just any book.

"I had it myself when I was young," said Hyrrokkin. "I realize you're not a giant, but the principles are the same. Just halve the ingredients in any of the shrinking spells or you'll end up tiny. But . . . you'll need to practice. Some of these spells are not straightforward. Some require ingredients you will have to travel many days to gather. Some require much study to understand and perform correctly."

"So what you're saying is the present you gave me is . . . homework?" I sighed.

Hyrrokkin let out a deep, throaty laugh.

"Well . . . thank you. I suppose." I narrowed my eyes at her.

"Just promise not to bring about the end of the world with it?" said Hyrrokkin.

"Oh, I can't possibly promise that," I said.

She gave me a look that could melt a glacier.

"I'll do my best," I said.

"Your best is all I want, Loki," she said.

"Well, clearly, my best is amazing, because you gave me a gift to celebrate my excellence."

Hyrrokkin shook her head. "No, Loki. You still have far to go and a lot to learn. This gift isn't a reward."

"It isn't? Then what is it?" This was very puzzling.

"We're a family," said Hyrrokkin. "Families do nice things for each other. Even if they don't really deserve it."

"But we're not a real family," I objected.

"Aren't we?" asked Hyrrokkin. "I don't think anyone but family could annoy me as much as you."

When we got home, Georgina and Valerie started doing some drawings of horses as we waited for their parents.

Thor sidled up to me. "So," he said. "I got you a present."

I cringed away. Usually when Thor says that, he farts on my head.

But he laughed. “No, not like that. A real one.” He passed me a very badly wrapped package. It looked like a sword. My heart sunk. I don’t want to do MORE fighting. I want to do less. Or preferably none. But as I held it, I felt a hum. This was a magical object. Perhaps an enchanted sword that did the fighting for me?

I opened it and it was not a sword. It was a wand.

A magic wand.

“Your understanding of magic helped us to defeat the giants. So maybe magic isn’t just an evil tool of the giants after all.”

“This is . . . actually very thoughtful.” I gazed down at the wand. *My* wand.

“It was Hyrrokkin’s idea, to go with the book,” said Thor, blushing. “But I went to retrieve it at great peril from a seeress. She made me perform many tasks which I will not speak of.”

I made a mental note to find out in *detail* all about *that* later on.

“You did a quest . . . for me?” I asked.

Thor shrugged.

I held the wand and felt its power. Thor had his hammer, and now I had a precious possession of my own.

"You do realize, that if I return to my evil ways, you might have just given me the tools to bring about the Apocalypse all on my lonesome?" I said, swishing the wand back and forth and thinking about all the spells I could do with it.

"Don't worry, fake brother," said Thor. "I'll be here to stop you."

I swished my wand again, and looked over to where Valerie and Georgina were giggling together as they drew pony after pony. And instead of a stab of jealousy, I felt something else.

I was happy that they were happy.

Well, that will *never* do. I am not a sap! I am not soft! I demand to return to my evil ways this *minute*.

! Be careful what you wish for, Loki . . .

THE END . . .
FOR NOW
#1

Acknowledgments

Thanks to all the gods and heroes at Walker, from the mighty sales team to the cunning language-shifting tricksters in rights, the magical production team, and the marvels of mythical proportions in marketing and publicity.

KAREN LAWLER . . . The Best Wife for All Eternity

MOLLY KER HAWN . . . Agent of Asgard

NON PRATT . . . Word God

LINDSAY WARREN . . . Word God Over the Water

JAMIE HAMMOND . . . Art God

KIRSTEN COZENS . . . She of the Publicity Pantheon

KAREN COEMAN . . . A Most Righteous God

RACHEL FATUROTI . . . God of Surnames

MAJA BACKVALL . . . Mystical Keeper of the Runes

SAMANTHA-LOUISE HAYDEN . . . God of Wisdom

TEAM SWAG . . . Emotional Support Horses

FEMINISM 2.0 . . . Mortally Insightful Women

ALICE, HELENA, AND VICKY . . . Mighty Valkyries

DAVID AND ROBIN . . . Dog-Adjacent Deities

ABBIE AND ELIZABETH . . . Black Hole Norns

HELEN TAMBLYN . . . Victim of Willful Joke Theft. Stealing jokes is what Loki would want.

IMOGEN RUSSELL-WILLIAMS . . . God of Chips

Oh, woe is me, I hear you cry!
You have finished this amazing book!
But fear not. I have another one coming!
It contains . . .
A school play
Temptation
Jewelry
Oh, and a handsome god who *gasp* isn't me!
Loki: A Bad God's Guide to Ruling the World
I'll be back!

LOKI
A BAD GOD'S GUIDE

Moral improvement takes more than one book. Don't miss out on all of Loki's (mis)adventures!

○ **BOOK 1**

Loki: A Bad God's Guide to Being Good

○ **BOOK 2**

Loki: A Bad God's Guide to Taking the Blame

About the Creator

LOUIE STOWELL started her career writing carefully researched books about space, ancient Egypt, politics, and science, but eventually lapsed into just making stuff up. She is the author of the Kit the Wizard series; the Loki: A Bad God's Guide series is her first project as both author and illustrator. The former publisher of Ladybird Books, Louie Stowell now writes full-time in London, where she lives with her wife, Karen; their dog, Buffy; and a creepy puppet that is probably cursed.